REMNANTS

REMNANTS

a novel

SAM HILL

iUniverse, Inc.
Bloomington

Remnants

This is a work of fiction. All of the characters, names, incidents, organizations, and dialogue in this novel are either the products of the author's imagination or are used fictitiously.

iUniverse books may be ordered through booksellers or by contacting:

iUniverse
1663 Liberty Drive
Bloomington, IN 47403
www.iuniverse.com
1-800-Authors (1-800-288-4677)

ISBN: 978-1-4759-4984-1 (sc)
ISBN: 978-1-4759-4985-8 (e)
ISBN: 978-1-4759-4986-5 (dj)

Library of Congress Control Number: 2012916885

Printed in the United States of America

iUniverse rev. date: 9/19/2012

This work is dedicated to my grand-father
and to my parents, whose wit, wisdom and
support helped make this book possible.

one

The first few gentle piano chords of the song resonated softly from the jukebox. James closed his eyes and motionlessly traced the notes in the musky air. A scent of pinewood gently tingled his senses in a way that he could very nearly taste as he listened quietly to the music. It was usually one of his favourite songs, but on this occasion it did not evoke the sentimentality that it once had.

A change had occurred, and everyone felt it. They took it with them everywhere they went. It was a weight in the pit of their stomachs. It was in the emptiness of their homes and the eerie quiet of the morning. The still machinery; the fuzzy, blank television; the hollow, monotonous bleep of the telephone. It was in the deserted roads and in the echoing bell tower of a vacant city hall. It was in the empty park swing and the vacant stares of those left behind. But most of all, the change was felt by a ringing, pervading emptiness. It was a loneliness that encompassed every aspect of the remnant's life. The liquor had not softened the blow or numbed the pain, for James at least. Rather it had shaped it, crafted it into something more precise that pricked his emotions and opened his mind to the condition that he found himself in, that they all found themselves in.

The music told of a beauty that was out of place in the dusty old tavern. It was a haunting and lonely beauty, one felt most profoundly in the dark night and in the quiet just before dawn, one felt best in the stillness of the morning, when the crickets have fallen silent and the birds have yet to begin their morning song.

As the song quickened in its urgency, a sombre voice whispered a tale of the flight of two young lovers. As James strained to listen, the words seemed to paint a picture of a frightening intimacy and a love distant to the experience he felt at that moment. He felt a sense of desperation as the song progressed, the once profound connection he associated with the music passing him by.

But this feeling soon passed.

Sighing, James opened his eyes and rubbed them with the heels of his hands. Gently rocking back on his stool, he looked around the bar, and the blurred plethora of images settled for the briefest second into a single picture before he again drifted away into his memories, far from the tavern.

Slow dancing in the dark on the beach at Taylor's Brook. He was swaying with Danielle in the crackling firelight, feeling like the last desperate lovers beneath the stars in the planet's final moments. During those days no words were necessary; it was a feeling beyond description. It was a passion that need not be spoken.

James caught his breath, and the image in his head shifted.

This time they were in the motel together, the one just off the dirt road in Parsonage. As James sat in the filtering dust of the twilight tavern, he smiled a distant smile long departed. Long ago, she had lain there like an angel, with her head upon his chest. In the present, tears of faithlessness welled in his eyes.

James steadied himself. Like the music, these memories were a still, soft beauty that demanded solitude. And with that realisation, the dreams departed from his head as wistfully as they had floated in, and he was left with the reality of the bar.

He rubbed his eyes again, producing deep red half circles above his flushed cheeks. The initial confusion that he had felt at the events of the past few days had turned into an echoing longing. A deep desire sprung from simmering frustration as he sat there that night.

The tavern. A familiar place, in a strange time.

The tavern was a stone building which was supported by long wooden beams climbing to a triangular roof and its simple interior looked scarcely fitting for a bar. Inside it was modestly lit by a series of candles that danced quietly in the dark, perched on black circular ceramic trays. Running along both sides of the building was a series of booths that were composed of rectangular tables between long, thin wooden benches with scarlet cushions placed upon them. Splitting the dual rows of booths was a floor thinly littered with a smattering of sawdust that ran from sturdy double oak doors, directly along the centre of the tavern to the bar itself.

The bar was a small, square shack-like structure, behind which stood racks of multiple drinks – clear bottles of dark green, ruby red, and clear fluids put unevenly upon rickety-looking shelves. Underneath this variety of nectars were stacked half a dozen enormous oak barrels, carefully placed side by side, their round face pointed towards the doors.

Tonight, the bar was tended by Rachel – a slender lady, pale in complexion, with striking, thin, blood-red-coloured lips that curved slightly downwards, complementing her narrow, hunched shoulders. She stood leaning against the side of the bar, a stained tea towel in her hand, absentmindedly rubbing a scratched pewter tankard, her light brown eyes distant and seemingly unfocused upon anything nearby.

She is sad, James thought, and a pang of unhappiness for her plight pricked him. *Sad, lonely too, perhaps.*

He was sitting on a stool in front of the bar. Every time James moved, the uneven stool rocked back and forth and he had to steady himself on the bar causing his back to arch away from the door behind him.

The noise in the tavern was low tonight with only intermittent and barely audible murmurs produced. James turned and looked around. The same faces, worn and tired, preoccupied, worried, afraid, occupied the booths as they had done last night and the night before.

They have lost their direction, James thought, *and who could blame them?*

Outside the wind rose, blustering and battering against the tavern walls, whistling furiously. The hairs on James' arms prickled, and he loosened his shoulders before shuddering involuntarily. Again he looked around at his fellow patrons, most of whom, like him, had wandered sadly to the bar for the last few nights.

Why had they come here?

There were no answers, nor solace in this place. No comfort was to be found in this dark night, or in any others – of that James was sure. He turned back to the bar, musing to himself. Perhaps they came out of some sense of instinct, maybe the yearning for human touch, however sparse and cold. Maybe, like himself, they felt as if they had no other place to go. Their homes no longer offered comfort, the warmth that defined a sense of home had been cut. It had been taken, from all of them, and they were cast adrift from everywhere and everyone.

And there were still no answers. They knew what James knew: the world did not belong to them anymore. Someone, or something, had taken it from them. It was someone else's now, whoever they were. On some level, they all knew this.

A profound, frightening solitude that was empty of joy marked life in these tumultuous days.

James cupped his drink with both hands, swilling the remaining froth in the base of the glass. He closed his eyes tightly and replayed the events of three days previously once again in his head. The song drifted away amid declarations of pious, unrequited love, and so its beauty departed with it. The candles flickered and James strained to remember.

two

here was not too much to remember in terms of clear details. That was part of the powerlessness. It had happened in a twinkling of an eye, unseen and unchecked. He had happened to be in the park when the event occurred, slowly chewing on his lunch.

Ten minutes previously, the red hands of the circular white clock had finally struck two thirty. The fluorescence panelled light of the shop lit the small area below where James toiled, waiting for time to slip out of the window and bring the day's end, or at least its lunch hour.

The work that was his charge was straightforward – tedious but simple. James whiled away his shift, tapping and tinkering with wristwatches, performing standard repairs, changing batteries, adjusting bracelets. The shop's income was modest but adequate and was hungrily consumed by a red-faced gentleman named Gerald who owned the store. This was a man whose greed was not matched by his work ethic, for Gerald was rarely seen.

But this absence did not unduly concern James. In fact, he preferred to be left alone in the store. In such solitude, he could escape into an exotic world or experience simple intimacy described so vividly by the words and imagination of others.

The occasional customer, pulling James from his books and back into the American Midwest, was few and far between and he seemed in his own mind to be in Cedar Falls for only the briefest time it took to serve them and repair their watch. The rest of the shift was spent in a daydreamed fantasy land far away from where he sat.

That late August day was clement; the final of throes of summer were gliding away before the harsh winter arrived and a mild breeze was whispering through the town as many of the visitors to the arcade rolled up their sleeves as they shopped, chatted and sipped coffee. Some wandered carefree, their coats casually slung over their shoulder. The college girls bounced around in short dresses, giving their legs a last public airing before taking out the thermals and gloves.

The shift was passing by, edging gradually towards his regular break of around 2:30. Business was quiet today. People were outside and that was where James was planning to head. When the time finally came, he clasped the shutter key in one hand and took his sandwiches and a creased sign that read *Back in an Hour* (complete with half-hearted and insincere apology) in the other and opened the hatch. James then stepped into the small square area that constituted the shop floor and walked the few short yards past the small selection of watches, silently praying that no customer would delay his lunch.

He made it the short distance outside, relieved.

After turning the key, the shutter slowly and nosily shuddered down, signalling the closing of the shop for the duration of his break. James was exhilarated at his brief escape into the sunshine and he moved quickly.

He placed the sign on the dusty black shutter, jamming it on crookedly with dirty blue tack before he moved off, keeping his head down as he made his way towards the exit. He passed the cookie stand nervously glancing at the girl behind the counter who sometimes visited him in the store. On this occasion, Gabriella was busy, her back to the arcade walkway, and James hurried on by unacknowledged. His shoes clicked on the empty marble-coloured floors as he turned the corner past the jewellers.

The two middle-aged ladies who worked at the jewellers wore deep, even dramatic makeup with pointed eyeliner and furious blusher that gave them an animated appearance. They were always pleasant to James, often dropping by the store with simmering cups of coffee, after which they would stay for a little chat, usually leaving with a smile and a kind word. Today they were sitting down lounging on comfortable-looking chairs. James returned their wave and continued towards the glass doors where the brightness of the outside world awaited.

He pushed the dark wooden bar that crossed the centre of the door and stepped outside onto an orange bricked surface and into a square. The area outside the arcade was enclosed on two other sides. There was *Harry's* restaurant on the left, its red neon sign of joined up writing turned off in the day. It was constructed from sandy-coloured brickwork that encased a large window, the tip of which was pushed open to let in the warm afternoon air. Directly in front of the door that James had passed through was the back of the vast smooth, pale grey stone building that served as the city hall, in front of which was a pool of blue water. In the centre was an elaborate foundation adorned by small nymphs spraying water into the air.

Only a small amount of sunlight made it through into the square, glimmering off the water adding to the bright warmth of the day and offering a brilliant dazzling effect to those who passed along the area. The fountain was gushing clear blue water into a shallow rectangular pool. The fluid sprinkled into the centre and onto a ceramic mosaic, which was made from pixelated blue and white square tiles upon a deep red background. This was complemented on either side by two large silver coins, each of which had etched upon them a solemn-looking gentlemen in a wig staring at each other unblinkingly.

The splashing water echoed around the square as James walked across the brickwork and made his way down a narrow alley between the corner of city hall and the side of the restaurant. The passageway was tight and the floor was an uneven grey cement. He hurried along the path, and the thin streaks of sun exploded into a bright light as he emerged into an area that stretched out before the gateway of the park marking the threshold of his destination.

A waist high red fence encased the luscious green fields beyond, and James entered the park beneath a curved red archway, as he stepped upon a soft, well-trodden yellow grass pathway.

Given the pleasant weather, the park was predictably busy that afternoon. Couples were idly pushing prams around, while others were strolling hand in hand lazily across the paths and fields, slowly enjoying themselves and each other. It was not a day for rushing, but James was eager to capture every second of his break, so he moved purposefully along the track.

Glancing around he saw a couple of college kids – a young brunette, who only had eyes for a distant-looking fellow opposite her, was sitting on the grass taking food from a wicker basket and together they sipped red wine. Another few teenagers were casually tossing a Frisbee around. Soon the schools would be out and the park would be full of rampaging children happily playing baseball and tag.

James broke off from the main track, taking a right towards some longer grass. Shin high yellow strands were swaying in the breeze, and he could hear them bristle as he approached. He ran his rough fingers through the dry strands, brushing them together as he moved towards a small lake that stood on the edge of the park.

On the far side of the water, large green trees surrounded the lake. Their leaves displayed a variety of orange, yellow, and red that floated in the air swinging gently from side to side as they silently fell through the air towards the still water.

This part of the park was not so busy, and James chose a bench to sit down on. It was a chipped green seat placed upon the crushed yellow track and from here, he could look to his right across the meandering path that wound its way towards the park entrance, or he could gaze the other way over the taller grass, the fields beyond and those young lovers who were picnicking upon it.

As a dragonfly buzzed around the bench, James reached for his sandwiches and pulled them from an air sealed bag. They were filled with ham and cheese, layered between two slices of white bread. He had neglected to bring his book, preferring instead to leave that for what promised to be the slow plod of the afternoon hours in the store. Today he wanted to enjoy the sights and the sounds of this late summer day and the whims of his own wandering imagination. He breathed in deeply, taking in the sweet smell of freshly cut grass, and wondered idly to himself whether this would be the last time that year that he would smell such a scent. Soon the weather would turn to rain and then snow.

He glanced at his watch. He had so little time, and the day was so pleasant.

James sighed and relaxed. Placing his sandwich on his lap, he stretched his arms out and fleetingly attempted to smooth the creases in his poorly ironed black shirt. Slumping his shoulders, he brushed the crumbs from his chest and continued on with his dinner.

A little girl was running around the side of the lake, chasing the floating leaves. She had a small pink hat that flapped down past her eyes. The girl, who wore a blue polka dot dress and who could not have been older than two, gurgled happily as she bounced around with what James assumed was her mother, an attractive blonde who was smiling with delight at the infant. She was wearing white shorts showing long tanned legs and a low-cut pink top held up by two thin straps that kept slipping onto her shoulders.

James watched them with a smile and felt a slight pang that was not quite jealousy – more a kind of nostalgic longing for a life that he had never had. James felt a sense of regret, a wistful sorrow that was almost sublime but a sorrow nonetheless, even as it was felt with an intensity that he was almost grateful for.

He looked away, lost in thought. His daydreams brought him again back to the decision that he had made a long time ago. This was one that had recently become a preoccupation for him, although he did not know why. It was a choice that had seemed for so long to be right, though the more time passed the more he questioned it. However sure you are, he mused, you can never truly know the consequences of a choice until they reveal themselves. The outcome of life's really big decisions – those life-defining turning points – cannot be prepared for, no matter how much planning is made, or even if you see them coming. However certain you are of the correctness of the choice made, you also wonder about the life not chosen and the path not walked. James took a deep breath, unhappy with his conclusions.

How could I still love her after all this time? How could I, when all I wanted to do when we were younger was to run away from home and leave it all behind? How could I still feel such a longing for Danielle? But it was just the timing – that was why I left all those years ago. It was not, it was never, because of her. It was just that the time was wrong.

And then, as he sat there reminiscing, the world changed.

James sat facing the water, slowly eating his sandwich. The leaves continued to sail down from the trees on the far side of the lake. The long grass still bristled in the wind. The ripples on the water continued to spread outward towards the muddy bank.

James looked at the sky above and a chill ran through him, his hairs standing on end. A red tint had invaded the edges of the clouds and the blue sky had deepened to a swirling purple. The light dimmed with the darkened sky.

The clouds stopped rolling. The birds stopped singing and the air was still.

The little girl stopped running and turned her head. James looked back down; he looked back down and gazed into her blue eyes. The still, small girl looked at him with a solemn expression that seemed far in advance of her youth. The stare unnerved him. Her eyebrows narrowed, and the corners of her mouth turned slightly upward in a kind of half smile. It was not a smile of joy or pleasure but one of knowing, a smile that held a secret truth.

And with that, in the merest blink of an eye, the girl vanished. She was gone.

three

James soon realised that the little girl was not the only one who had disappeared. Neither were the anguished screams of the mother hers alone.

He sat still, staring unblinkingly at the spot where the girl had been looking at him. He was neither panicked, like her mother was, nor frozen to the spot.

He was just surprised.

Sitting there days later in the bar, it seemed strange to James that he was so ready to believe what had happened. His mind instantly accepted the truth of the matter – the little girl was gone. Where and why were other matters, and he could ascertain no facts in that area. He knew only that she was gone, and from the mounting hysteria behind him that day, James calmly deduced that others felt the same painful loss the child's guardian demonstrated so terribly.

He had to leave the park. Whatever he would do later, now he had to escape to somewhere else, and he did so without haste although somehow he knew that whatever damage there was to be wrought had already been done. The dreadful truth of the event was too late to be denied and the loss suffered was too late to be changed and it was not yet the time to wonder. He had to go. After this he was not sure, but he had to leave.

Slowly he rose from the bench and turned from the lake and fled the way he came.

James walked through the long grass and stepped onto the track. On either side of the walkway, the park fields displayed scenes of pandemonium. Those few people that remained were gripped by a manic frenzy. A man in shorts ran aimlessly, frantically yelling out a name that James could not make out. Heads twitched and James passed through the flailing limbs and desperate movements of the panic stricken.

He walked on turning the corner towards the park entrance amid the chaos. He kept his head down trying to drown out the hysterical noises, only glancing up to notice a girl beside the brick pillar, crouched underneath the arched sign that he passed through into the park in what seemed like an entire age ago.

She was a rosy cheeked teenager of about sixteen, with a deep crimson and amber school jacket draped over her shoulders, crying silent tears. She looked up at James through damp, saucer shaped eyes, almost pleading with him to do something, to make some sense out it. He stopped, looking down at her.

Of all the things that he saw that day, the memory of that girl was the most precise. That girl, that look, that desperate imploring gaze. He had nothing for her, he could not ease her pain, he could not help. A frantic thought told him to say something, say anything, think of something, offer something.

"I'm sorry." His voice was hoarse.

Was that all I could have said to her? The thought tormented, and she had almost laughed at him. *Could I find nothing else within myself to offer?*

He shook his head, dismayed at his utter inability to help, and hurried out of the park. The narrowly enclosed square scarcely offered more order than the fields, and a violent fight had broken out in front of the restaurant between two men in stripped shirts with matching red ties and slicked back hair. Punches were thrown and taken and blood had spilt onto the ground below, as the men tussled for room.

In those few moments there was rage, and noise, and sorrow, and despair, and denial, and hate.

An ear-splitting crash momentarily drowned out all of the other noises as a fragmented table flew through the restaurant window, landing amidst the shards on the square. A well-dressed bald man with tanned skin and a blue suit called in vain for calm, wringing his hands, imploring all before him to just stop it all.

Whilst some fought, others mourned in solitary acceptance, sitting still in the shadows of lonely corners. James moved passed them all and went into the arcade, avoiding the confrontations and the lonely prayers. The shopping area was deserted, but James felt some kind of overarching threat, confirmed by repeated sounds of nearby screams and high pitched whines of shop security alarms. He felt as if the floor itself was throbbing like a pulsating, seething tide beneath his feet.

Still James walked on and the source of the anarchy became apparent. The jewellers was unattended by workers, though a man in a grubby white vest glimpsed into view as James continued around the arcade. He was raising one of the chairs high above his head. As James walked on he heard glass crunch and more sirens sounding adding to the chorus.

James pressed on through the arcade and flinched as a young girl burst past him with a laptop under her arm, its security tags still wrapped around the hardware. He glanced at Gabriella's stall, but she was not there.

The rest of the walkway resembled a warzone. The marbled floor was littered with shards of glass and strewn clothing. Cries and screams rung out from somewhere close by yet out of sight.

Not knowing why he was returning, James opened the shutters to the shop, just enough for him to slide under, and he sat down on the only chair, a torn black seat whose back rest was permanently stuck at an uncomfortable arched angle.

He closed his eyes.

The little girl.

She was there and then she was not. That was what had happened. Just like that, a click of the fingers. Those facts were undeniable. He rubbed his eyes with the palm of his hands and felt older than his twenty-five years. He replayed the situation again. The little girl was there, gurgling happily, and then she was not. He saw the anguish on the woman's face, saw pain etched in the expressions of the girl by the gates. Beyond the rage of others, this was what he saw – woe. Real, wrenching, aching, miserable, frightened woe.

James thought back. He walked to work this morning. Even in the early hours it had been warm and he had left his coat behind. He had placed his iPod in his pocket to pass the forty-minute walk and had lost himself in harsh worlds and romantic melodramas of various tunes. He was so embarrassed by his taste in music that he had paused it when he passed the girl whose face he knew from the corner shop. He had half smiled at her, before he remembered that she was out of his league. She was too young, no older than nineteen, too fresh, too pretty, too nice. The day had been fine, sunny. It had been a nice day.

James forced himself to consider the fact of the matter. The little girl from the park had gone. From the chaos unfolding outside, it was clear that she was not the only one.

It was the truth of the matter. The reality as it is.

They had gone. He thought back. The sky had changed just before. It was as if those who occupied the heavens had clamoured forward for a grandstand view of the events. The clouds were purple, the air was still.

James could not shake a thought. The little girl knew. She knew something was happening. She knew she was leaving this place. He chided himself. That was a ridiculous assumption. He could not know that. He could not, but he felt it and it nagged at him.

Before long, his thought turned towards his mother. The all too familiar grief he had felt at her death pierced him again. Would she have known what had happened?

There was no way that she could. But he still wished that she was here. She would tell him what to do. She would sit him down and tell him that he was being silly. That people did not disappear for no reason. That somewhere, amid the chaos of the day, there was some explanation. Even if she could not find it, she would get on with it. She had got on with it all her life, never complaining, never working anything less than hard right up until the end.

She had explained her cancer with similar grit – methodically explaining the condition and its effects. She had calmly outlined that she believed in a kind and loving God, and a life beyond the bitter pain of her experience in this life.

But how would she have explained this?

James suddenly felt incredibly lonely. He had no girlfriend since he and Lindsey had broken up a few months ago. Back then, it seemed like it was for the best. Physically they had been close and they had enjoyed the pleasure of each other's bodies. But there was nothing to it. No deeper purpose or intimate plan beyond the moment. Even holding hands with her did not feel right. They had not interlocked or forged any kind of bond. But Lindsey was someone. She would text him, it was nonsense, but it was contact. It was confirmation that he was not completely alone.

That he was not alone like he was this night in the tavern.

He had not heard from Lindsey in a while, which was okay, except that he had not heard from anyone else either. James was angry at his selfish thoughts.

Is anyone wondering? Is anyone worried that I might be gone?

He mostly worked alone, before walking home to an empty house to watch quiet reruns of old comedy programmes. His nights were mostly spent in lonely reading, as he sought lost worlds amidst dreams of a life of significance.

In the most part he was content. He had never dated much. The experience with Danielle had done something to him. He had caught a glimpse of something with her. A life that, for once, he was not eager to escape.

But still he had left it behind.

He had made the choice and he had gone. The loss that he felt at the disappearances had not pressed down so profoundly upon him since his first night away from Danielle all those years ago in what now seemed both faraway and also achingly close. He recalled that first cold night apart, when every quiet voice in his head grew into a scream.

That day in the shop he had reached for the phone.

It was dead. There was no dial tone, no static. He checked the plug and the phone was as he left it. James flicked the receiver to no effect and with the same calm resignation that he had displayed earlier, he slumped back.

What would he do now?

Unanswered questions had flooded James' mind.

Were the disappearances localised to Cedar Falls? That was not likely, though he could not know for sure. For the first time he considered his own survival. Had he survived? Or had he missed out? Was he blessed or cursed, saved, or damned?

He did not know. He did not know. He did not know.

James felt jaded. Just outside the small area of his shop people were screaming and glass was breaking. Beyond that, in that decisive moment, the world had become different than it was before. He had never really understood theology or divine plans or anything like that, but even he knew that some new epoch had been ushered in an instant on that afternoon. The course of life had turned.

He leaned back on his chair and then, he was not alone.

Into the shop, sliding, scrambling, came Gabriella. James turned and looked at her and saw instantly the same helpless desperation that he felt. Gabriella wore with it a sadness that gave her a wearied expression.

James stood and moved toward her.

Gabriella was shaking. Her brown apron that was tied around her waist was torn, and her long brown hair was straggled and knotted. Her face had a deep red coloration and from the smudge on her mascara, he knew she had been crying.

"James!" Her tone was harsh as if she were looking for a fight. But there was defiance competing with shock and stubbornness battled her confusion.

"They tried to come for my stall. I hit them, but they kept coming and Jenny had just disappeared. The sweet shop is on fire, James. It is on fire. What are we going to do?"

He stood just in front of her quietly looking at her. Gabriella paused and hissed at him through gritted teeth.

"Don't just stand there. Give me your phone."

James stepped towards her and put his arms around her. She was six inches shorter, and his arms encased her. Gabriella stopped moving and the fight drained away from her. She buried her head into his chest and after a moment, she sobbed uncontrollably.

They stayed in that embrace for what seemed like an age before James finally pulled away and offered Gabriella the single seat behind the counter.

"My phone is not working. I can't call anyone."

"Our phone is out too."

"Jesus, what the hell has happened? What the hell …?" She trailed off.

That was three days ago and he remembered every detail. Every colour, sight, sound was there etched in his memory. He could feel every texture and smell every scent.

James had played it out in his head time and time again. He left the shop that day and walked Gabriella home. Outside the danger remained and people were angry and afraid. The initial rage still had not run its course. Ignoring the park, James had ushered her through the back streets and alleys, keeping their head down and staying close to one another. They had left the arcade through the fire doors, which took them onto a narrow fenced off pathway of crushed asphalt. The walkway was lined with trees, which shielded them from the fields and the wails beyond.

Having seen Gabriella safely home, James had politely turned down her offer to go inside. Despite his abiding loneliness, he still wanted to be alone. He left for his own house, taking a similar secluded path home, weaving through back alleys, barely daring to look up until he was at his door.

Sliding his key in and wriggling it until the flaky black door creaked open, James stepped into his front room.

He slumped onto his grubby sofa. The sun shone through the window, brightening the wooden panels on the floor. He sat there quietly for a moment. Usually when he came in, he would fix himself something to eat, usually some variety of pasta, a choice dictated by culinary ineptitude rather than personal preference.

But that evening he was not hungry.

James remembered that first evening after the event, sitting in the small damp house that was his home. He had reached for the phone more in hope than expectation and found it as redundant as the one in the shop and as useless as his television which that night was dead, resolutely refusing to show anything but a black background.

In the tavern James smiled to himself. He had not lamented the loss of the television that much, for it had still not returned. Neither had the phones or the Internet. Mankind had been truly cut off from each other.

The link was severed.

That first evening, James, in the utter absence of anything else, went to the tavern, where he had continued to spend his nights. Most people had not gone back to work and James was no exception. He had not seen his employer, so he had not heard from him.

James sometimes thought himself almost lucky that he had no family.

Sometimes he envied the pain of those who had been bereaved. They felt something other than directionless boredom. Their pain had a context. At least they had some focus to their plight and some direction for their grief.

James just had nothing to do. He had no plan or any idea of what to do next.

So he came to the tavern and he drank with the others.

four

the tavern stood on a hill, ancient and rustic, the destination of a long meandering path made up of cobbled misshapen stones tightly packed together. The modestly steep route that followed up the pine tree laden hill was lit by orbs of deep blue that were perched on top of a sturdy black pole which in other circumstances would have lent a gentle, even romantic ambience to those wandering upwards. In the late summer evening following the disappearances, James ascended the hill to a tap-tapping of woodpeckers and flies buzzing around the lights. He was not alone in his walk to the tavern, as he was joined by others who were also making the trek, slowly ambling upwards in silence.

The building itself was situated beyond a gravelled picnic area comprising of a clutch of wooden benches and flat, rectangular tables beneath an expansive parasol. The area would usually be busy on a pleasant night, though it was deserted that evening.

Beyond the outside seating area lay the pub itself. It was a building that seemed more in keeping with an English village rather than a small town in the American Midwest. The paint work was white, immaculately maintained, with large black supports running through it, crisscrossing the bobbled surface.

Hanging baskets containing vividly coloured drooping purple and red flowers hung either side of a black doorway. The curtains of the four – two up, two down – windows were all drawn, showing only the opposite side of what James knew to be red curtains. The slate roof slanted down to a row of spotlights that offered ample illumination for the front of the building, as its welcoming glow seemed to beckon the hilltop patrons.

As James wandered up that night, and each of the three days since the vanishings, the silence felt eerie and unsettling. The only real constant sound was a creaking, emanating from the swinging sign hanging in the centre of the inn, which depicted a black outline of a snake-like dragon lurking beneath a crescent moon and a scarlet background. The words above the image gave the name of the tavern – *The Serpent's Feet*.

Despite the Satanic overtones of its name, the tavern was a friendly place. Warm and intimate, James thought it was a good reflection of the people of Cedar Falls. He was not a regular customer – perhaps a couple of Saturdays and maybe three or four weekdays a month – but the landlady, a busty, rambunctious woman of infinitesimal good nature, was always welcoming to him. Sue was around fifty and was chatty and friendly to all who crossed her doors, often pouring their drink the second they entered the bar. The people of Cedar Falls, James thought, were generally happily set in their routines.

In his estimation, Sue must have been very attractive once, and there were still signs in the sparkle of her eyes and the playful curve of her mouth that glimpsed at her past as a heartbreaker. James liked the tavern because he could go there alone and chat away pleasantly with people he barely knew for an entire evening, sharing rounds and stories together. They would tease each other, listen to each other, talk to each other. To many it might have seemed boring, but he liked it. With people whose surnames he did not know, he listened to them grumble about work, speak fondly about their kids, and complain about wives or girlfriends. He would talk to them about his plans and his future. In the shimmering candlelight of the tavern, the talk around a foamy beer would be light and easy, stretching long into the night often well beyond what should have been closing time. Even so, James knew that for him, and he sensed that it was also for the others, whoever they may be, the idle chats were somehow important, even if their content was not.

James had so few friends in his new home, but when he went to the tavern, it seemed like this sad truth may not be so real after all. His awkwardness talking to strangers, his clumsiness with words ebbed away when he sat himself down on the smooth wooden stools in front of the bar. On the downside, when he finished drinking and he and his fellow patrons descended the hill and returned to their various homes, he opened that door to his empty house, and the hole always seemed gaping. When he lay alone in his bed, he felt how much he missed *her,* how much he missed the life he had chosen to forsake, and this would often take on a frightening and profound intensity that seemed inescapable before sleep took his thoughts and shifted them into an incoherent mess of dreams and visions.

But for those hours of understanding and empathy, for that human contact, James returned to the tavern repeatedly. When the disappearances had struck, and when he could find no solace anywhere else, he picked up his keys and wallet. Leaving the house, he turned the corner at the end of his street and walked the short distance beside the stream to the base of the hill. The blue lights had just flickered into life when he began the steady climb.

five

h e had returned to the summit of the hill on each of the three nights since the vanishings. Perhaps he had expected too much, but the whole atmosphere of the pub had altered, changing along with the world below.

The first and most obvious thing about the bar was that Sue was amongst those who had gone. James had never been there when Sue was not. He was used to her dropping her apron and pouring herself a drink, always a colourful fruity one, and throwing herself on a stool with her customers, cheerfully lambasting her barmaids and giggling with James and the other patrons.

Her absence was like a vacuum, sucking the air out of the tavern.

The laughter and playful murmur was also gone, replaced by a mood of isolated solitude that persisted as James' thoughts drifted back to the present. Still, no one had any answers. No reasons. It was pointless discussing it further with others apart from the initial details that people had professed that first night. Most had spoken of who had gone, and a few offered hope for their destination, believing that they had gone to heaven as the world was going to hell, but even that little chatter had soon drifted away. The lack of communications stifled any further discussion as no one had anything new to say.

The fact of the matter was that no one knew anything. With no knowledge, hope remained fleeting and salvation seemed impossible. What little comfort that existed was gleaned from being with each other in a kind of shared mood that swayed between bewilderment and misery, but comfort could not be found from any attempt at truth. The situation seemed too painful to speculate upon. Everyone had lost someone. No one joked about their wives nagging anymore or their children raising hell. Eventually people largely stopped talking and the numbers to the tavern had slowly dwindled.

Everyone had lost someone close – a wife, a mother, a boyfriend, a brother. Everyone, that was, except James. He had no one to lose.

He raised his eyes to Rachel, who turned sadly to him.

"A pint please, Rach." He said softly. "Take one for yourself if you want to."

Rachel smiled sadly and took his glass, the little finger of her hand slightly, involuntarily, stroking the tip of James' finger.

"Thank you, but I had better not. We are almost out."

His eyes widened in surprise. "Almost out?"

Rachel nodded. "There is no way of ordering anymore."

He looked at the young barmaid, scarcely out of her teens. She looked so tired, so sad. The burden was just too much for Rachel, for everyone. He smiled at her but could offer no words of support, nothing to even momentarily relieve the pain.

She handed him his drink and she returned his smile before retreating into her distant world. James began to sink the drink.

I need more than this. There has to be more than this. I have to leave this place.

He took his time over his drink, sipping it quietly with his head down. He assessed his options for the millionth time, concluding only one thing: though with more clarity than he had already worked out.

He had to escape this.

Polishing off the rest of the drink, he placed the empty glass onto the bar.

"Get out of here, Rachel. This is going to turn ugly when you run dry. Please get out of here."

Rachel smiled noncommittally. Finishing his drink, he turned for the door. His exit elicited no response and no one in the tavern stirred. James stepped into the warm night air, unsure of where to go and what to do. A simple walk was the extent of his plan, and he began the drop into town.

The sky was black, sprinkled with a dazzling array of stars that pinpricked the night air with a sparkling and ethereal glow. The warm air around him was tinted blue from the lamp stands.

The gentle chirp from concealed crickets was the only sound that James could hear as he slowly wandered the winding track back down into Cedar Falls. The soft calm of the twilight hour granted him a serenity that he had scarcely thought possible, as he observed the surroundings of the small town that had become his home.

Cedar Falls was once a thriving mountain town built around a modest-sized timber industry. Prospectors from the East Coast had settled in the area, finding its warm summers and only mildly harsh winters pleasant if not luxurious. Around the borders of the town, wealthy industrialists built large white mansions, mixing with the ranchers whose homestead lay between Cedar Falls' shapely hills and deep gorges. These settlements were sparsely placed in the midst of an expansive forest of pine, which was dissected by a wide river teeming with trout and salmon.

All that separated the vast luscious wilderness from the town was a single suspension bridge that allowed for a sole lane of traffic each way and a pedestrian walkway by the side. The town itself was shaped like a diamond. On the far side of the town, on the opposite side to the bridge, was the hill that James descended. Cedar Falls was like a secluded island standing in the middle of a river, and though the roads about the Falls were wide and plentiful, there was only one viable exit, on one side of town. The isolated nature of the settlement had granted the folk of Cedar Falls a measure of pride at their town's wholesomeness. Far away from the sin of the outside world, the town was seen by its residents as a final bastion of goodness in a decaying world. It was a remnant of a disappearing world, a last slice of a rustic and rural Americana, and like many island folk, they were proud of their homeland.

On the whole, James had quickly decided that Cedar Falls was a decent place to live. It had a genuine community whose local council was made up of people whom everyone knew. Even James recognised them about town. Meetings in the town hall were typically haphazard, with the speaker addressing members of the floor by their first name as they solved simple problems like fixing the faulty streets lights on Arklay Road and debating whether the town benches were going to get painted again this year. The pace of life was slow, and people took their time with each other. Shoppers chatted to checkout girls, and old men played leisurely games of bridge in the park.

James felt that he was being slowly accepted, even though he was an outsider from the distant state of Maine. The sheriff, a gruff but honest and generally pleasant man named David, stopped by to talk to him at work from time to time, as did one or two others.

Despite his fondness for Cedar Falls, James was a little lonely there since he had left Danielle. It was a loneliness that crept up on him, regularly betraying his sense of well being, invading his thoughts without warning or indication, lingering seemingly indeterminately. Then, as elusively as it would arrive, so it would depart just as quietly.

That sense of solitude remained at bay as he passed the estate in which he lived and, instead of going home, he took the main route towards the town centre. Life in Cedar Falls had changed since its establishment in the eighteen hundreds, and the evidence was all around him. The money in the timber industry had begun to run dry at the turn of the century as new territories continued to open up and the town had been forced to adapt, which it had done capably. Cedar Falls was lucky. The money the industrialists made from logging was poured back into the area, apparently out of genuine affinity for the town, or so James had read in *Cedar Falls: A Life*, a brief town biography given to him by Mrs Grocott, the old lady he lived next to and whose rubbish James carried out on Tuesday nights.

Businesses sprang up slowly, and a new mall was built in the 1960s. It was not flashy or slick, James thought, but it was functional. The town invested money in its college, which paid dividends by retaining at least a measure of the students that graduated from either one of the town's two high schools. Cedar Falls was not an affluent area, but neither was it deprived. It had survived due to hard work and opportunism, and James thought that in general, the people were happy. The community spirit was strong and people got by with a smile and a chat.

James' wandering took him to the very centre of the town.

The middle of Cedar Falls harked back to its inception, heavily influenced by Lutheran settlers. The geographical centre was a square of grass – usually neatly trimmed – that stood in the middle of the town's commerce. The turf was enclosed by middle-sized buildings of orange brick work that made up the arcade standing either side of the faded white marble of Cedar Fall's town hall. The scene was completed by a row of mostly redundant older wooden shacks that preserved the frontier history of the town, providing the occasional tourist and local enthusiasts with a modest historical society chronicling the life of the Falls.

James approached the centre and chose a bench at the head of the lawn that looked across the grass and thought again about the events of the previous few days.

As he sat in the solitary silence of the evening, the full moon shone brightly, looming large above him. The slight incline of the field made the moon seem larger than usual and as he looked at it, he seemed to see every crater of earth's eternal companion. He was no expert on astronomy, at least not in terms of knowing the names of the constellations, but as he sat looking at the giant satellite above the earth that radiated a soft yellow light upon the land below, he felt a feeling of awe, and after a time, a sense of clarity succeeded his wonder.

As the evening passed the witching hour and entered early morning, the streets were deserted. The town still bore the occasionally brutal scars of the vanishings, as no one had made any effort to clear it up. He thought of the cars that he had seen that lay strewn across the road, their drivers departed, their passengers often deceased. This self-evident truth only found a home within his understanding as he sat there. People were dead, people were gone. That was the fact of the matter. His only choice was what he would do now.

The moon shone, as did the stars above. James looked at it and once again felt that unexpected serenity. The evening was gentle, and he was almost content. As the temperature dropped in the still, lonely cool before dawn, James sat looking across the green. Directly in front of him was the city hall. The building was styled like an ancient Greek temple, with a small flight of steps leading to three large imposing pillars that stood before the civic centre beyond. Behind the building, to the left, was a large bell tower made up of dark red brickwork that led up to an open platform containing an enormous copper bell. Above this platform was a circular white clock with black Roman numerals beneath a triangular roof. Both the city hall and the bell tower were amply lit with sequenced orange lights that chased upward lending a sense of majesty and grandeur that seemed to James to be an overshoot of the usual modesty of Cedar Falls.

He sat in the centre of town and he was struck again by the quietness. There were no people milling around, no revellers, no giggling couples holding hands. There were no cars, no planes overhead. There were no dogs barking, no distant music.

There was nothing at all.

Nothing except James and his thoughts and the recurring question. *How had it come to this?*

six

James stretched out his arms and legs wearily causing them to noisily crackle. Glimpses of the life he had already lived had quietly sneaked into his head uninvited but regularly since he moved to Cedar Falls. A memory he had presumed lost often sprang up at the most unexpected times. He would be drifting along a supermarket aisle pushing a trolley or standing in a queue in the post office, and without bidding he would remember one of Danielle's expressions, a slight smile or murmur in her sleep perhaps. Sometimes it was simply some departed inkling of an intensity of feeling he had once felt for her.

Whenever this occurred, James would work hard to press it down into his gut. He would always do so with the promise to himself that he would revisit the memory at some more appropriate point. Late at night, alone in his bed under his sheets, he would resolve to try and recapture the feeling – the emotion, the look – but he was never quite able to with the same colours and textures. The memories came and went of their own accord, visiting unbidden or not at all.

As he sat fragile and alone on the bench this night, James' memory again showed his mind a glimpse of his time with Danielle and on this occasion he did not suppress the image as he allowed it instead to bloom. Soon his mind filled with a random series of images and emotions that he struggled to place into a narrative. Supplementing the rich emotion of the memory with the cold reason of what had happened, James pictured the time when it was he who had done the disappearing.

The story of him and Danielle was a tale of normal, everyday teenage love. It was the very same tale that played out for millions of other people that means little to anyone else.

They had met at the college they both attended in Little Pickering, Maine. It was not love at first sight, at least not for James. Rather, it had sneaked up upon him, barely noticeable until it had fully and surprisingly blossomed. The course of their love had run smoothly, perhaps even boringly. Before this realisation, and after his awkward mumblings, they had gone out one evening around Pickering town.

The more they got to know each other, the more the flower in both of their hearts bloomed. Soon they reached a comfortable point where being with the other was enough, and the will James had to constantly try to impress her with claims of the drama and escapades of his own life had moved into a pleasant enjoyment of her company.

Eventually one winter's night when the moon was full and footsteps crackled on frosty ground, James had walked Danielle home, softly holding her hand as snow began to fall. As the cold snap lent a freshness to the air, they reached her door. Her soft brown eyes meeting his, she had invited him inside. Dying embers snapped on an open fire and the wind howled outside, shuddering at the windows. Danielle slowly, tentatively, peeled off his layers. Tenderly, they traced the curves of each other's bodies before they made gentle love in her bedroom. In a comfortable embrace, they then quietly dozed off.

The next morning he lay awake as the red sun slowly peeked through the window, producing the first light of dawn. Thin rays of sunlight crept between the narrow gaps in the curtains of Danielle's room onto her warm, thick duvet, which was snugly entwined around their bodies.

Behind the house, the sound of water trickling down a brook continued as robins sweetly twittered outside the window. On that morning, James had looked at the sleeping girl beside him and felt a calm measure of happiness and a feeling that he was somehow home.

It had snowed all night, and it continued for a day, and a night, and a day.

Their winter's love passed unhindered into spring when they would sometimes get caught walking in the rain and they would hurry and splash around in the mud. The morning chorus of robins moved into the cluck of chicks. The scent of freshly cut grass again soothed the nostrils and the days grew longer and the sun warmer.

One morning, as rays of light sneaked through the window ever earlier, a storm brewed and began to flash on the horizon. As time ticked onwards, the storm began to move towards the warmth and towards where they lay.

The night was deepening as James sat on the square. It was the first time he had really been able to look back at his time with Danielle. It was the only time that he had put together all the pieces into one. For so long he had suppressed everything that he was playing back, though he knew it must seem modest to an outsider. Each time he conjured the memories, something would shut them down, and though he would make a point of returning to them later, he never could conjure them again.

But now every sight, every smell, every word and every feeling was returning. He felt as if his body was becoming reanimated after years of being dormant. Though the memories were painful, James was grateful. In the early hours, under a plethora of stars and the bright throbbing street lamps of Cedar Falls, he was thankful for his sorrow.

He was finally feeling something, the nature of which was almost unimportant. What was certain was that no feeling he could evoke was more pronounced than that of the unhappiness of his and Danielle's parting. The pictures came flooding back with all the clarity of today's events. James closed his eyes and replayed another scene, remembering the construction of his escape.

Since his mother died when he was fifteen, James had plotted to leave Little Pickering behind. The town no longer held him in the thrall that it had done when he was a child and he vowed never to depart. The time when he thought himself content of a life lived beside the town football stadium and eating hot dogs everyday was long gone by his late teens.

James had thrown himself into university applications, eagerly viewing every institution he could before choosing one hundreds of miles away, in Illinois. With its modest academic program it was no Ivy League institution, but it was the perfect fit for him. It was a place where he would be able to get accepted into with ease over accomplishment.

He had eagerly discussed it with all his friends and as the year advanced, the dream got closer and the escape plan took shape. He had visited open days, viewed his history syllabus expounding the horror of the crusades and the mysticism of ancient dreamers. James fantasised about solving the mystery of Kublai Khan's lost fleet, of wandering freely across campus, of dorm rooms and experiencing sights and sounds that he could not even imagine. He dreamt of finding treasure and of changing the world. He dreamt of a life far from Little Pickering.

But Danielle was a hometown girl. Her large family all lived in Little Pickering, as had generations before her. Danielle's attachment was strong and she was happy there and content and fulfilled, she had never really thought of leaving.

James' escalating excitement at his impending departure had upset her. With strong love came sharp pain. He remembered her eyes welling with tears as he spoke of where he was soon to live. James had thus decided not to talk about it around her. It had hurt him that he believed the source of Danielle's unhappiness was the idea that she thought James wanted to leave her behind.

That was not true. It wasn't.

He loved her. He wanted to be with her. But he was to leave, that was his plan; that was his destiny. Now years later, the self-serving nature of how he thought seemed so apparent, and he scarcely believed himself capable of such selfishness. Thinking back, He knew his reluctance to even broach the subject of Illinois around Danielle stifled any discussion of options. There was no talking of a long-distance relationship. The idea was alien to him anyway. He and Danielle were too close in some ways. James knew could not be with Danielle without being close to her.

The smile on her face, her expression of concentration as she nibbles her pen, I could not miss that. Better to make a clean break.

Alongside the picture of a dramatic life of adventure and intrigue, James also dreamed of a simple life that he would share with Danielle in a cosy house, where he would wait with a warm cup of tea ready for her when she walked back home in the cold evening after Tuesday-night aerobics. He wanted to cuddle up to her on her soft brown sofa and watch nonsense on television and listen to her talk about her day. He wanted to smile and giggle with her. But James had also other dreams that could not be satisfied in this way, and ultimately he had already made his choice before meeting Danielle.

But James knew he could not ask her to go with him, just as she knew that she could not ask him to stay. They avoided the issue and delayed the conversation and time ebbed away. Like cupping his hands to catch sand leaking from an hourglass, James just could not hold on. Months passed. The shorter time got, the more desperate he became, and yet more time slipped quietly by.

However, they finished their final college exams and a long summer stretched before them. Together they went hiking in the Conifer Forest, sleeping under the stars and between the pines. They swam in the cool lagoon and had picnics in the park.

Then arrived the inevitable conversation two weeks before he was due to leave. Seated in the corner of a cafe they frequented during free periods of college, James cupped his hands around a simmering cup of coffee and Danielle stirred a mug of hot cocoa, her spoon clinking across the smooth pottery. They calmly, painfully talked it out. James' memory fogged on this meeting. Some things, he guessed, were just too hurtful to dredge up. They spoke of their love for one another and they let each other go.

He left her in tears that evening. Mournful, sorrowed but defiantly stifled sobs accompanied his departure. James walked out of the cafe and went home to bed. That night he felt as if he was a thousand years old.

Over the next two weeks he kept himself busy preparing for his move and trying not to think of Danielle, though she never strayed far from his thoughts.

He did not see Danielle until the night before he left, when he met her for one final time, one last evening of intimate togetherness. In their last moments of tenderness, James professed himself ready to give it up. He was ready to give it all in for her. To lay aside his hopes and dreams and live just for her, because all the promise of his glorious future could not meet the glory of Danielle's love. With her he was someone, without status, without money, he was still someone. He would give it up, everything, for her.

Smiling sadly, she kissed his lips and told him to go, and leave he did. That was nearly four years ago and James had not seen her since, though he often thought of her. He did not know if he would see her again, but at that moment, sitting on that bench on that evening, he decided to try.

The pain was profound, even years later and hundreds of miles away, James still felt it. It was like a grip that was tugging his organs inwards. However, he knew that his years at university had been amazing. He had fun, expanded his mind, felt himself mature as he realised the nature of his personality, and made close friends he still kept in contact with and who he saw at occasional reunions. He discovered and accepted true responsibility by living on a budget and making his own choices accordingly. There was always something going on, someone around the communal area of their dorm at all hours of every day. For the first two months they had no television at all and James scarcely missed it.

But he did miss Danielle, and at times he felt very lonely. Those first nights without her were cold and lonesome. There was no warm touch in the dark, no sound of gentle breath beside him.

Separation from her at first drew their hearts still closer, while frustration at their distance inflamed their passions even more. They became more abandoned from themselves somehow. He was less in control of his emotions as they spoke on the telephone and in the pages of letters that they wrote to each other. It became no longer easy and their love had become something of a torment. In those days, James was tired, and thinking of such sweet things as Danielle became burdensome and heavy, greatly saddening his spirit, causing him to drift away from reality into daydreams of her touch.

James kept the letters that they had exchanged in that first year of their parting, because they had provoked such emotions. Though it was painful, whilst James was denied her presence, at least through her words some sweet semblance of herself remained with him.

Their letters grew increasingly sad and desperate as time passed. Though both had it in their power to remedy each other's grief, neither removed it. Their lives, it seemed, had passed each other by, their time together had been spent. It became more difficult to remember what they had felt beyond the sorrow at their spilt and the continued pain at their distance. Over time, a new thought began to invade the old dream of Danielle, forcing him to interrupt or abandon his recollection of the past. He stopped thinking about her as much as he could, forcing her away from his thoughts. Over time, James was able to see something funny without wondering if Danielle would find it funny too. He could receive good news or become excited without feeling the overwhelming desire to tell her.

Eventually, he could no longer remember what her lips felt like on his. He learned to stop thinking of Danielle while looking at other women and she went from an hourly thought to a daily picture to a weekly musing before becoming a monthly image. Then, finally, she became nothing more than an aching memory and an unprompted dream that came and went at random intervals.

His time at university finished and James took a job in Cedar Falls, working for a small watch repair company. It was a position far away from the greatness that he believed would be his, and his new employment seemed to fit part of his post-university funk. Whilst he was without Danielle at university, at least he was having fun most of the time. When he graduated, this was no longer the case. The promised greatness never emerged. Neither did the genuine significance that seemed to constantly beckon throughout his early adulthood. People seemed to take joy in telling him that he was in the 'real world' now.

That night sitting on the bench, when James was left with just himself and the memory of a life that he had not lived, he realised that he was unhappy. He did not like his job, and the relationships he had had since Danielle were fleeting and unfulfilling, never seeming to last beyond a superficial burst.

Danielle was more than a girl. She was a bridge between a dead-end job and a time when he believed that the greatness promised to him was just around the corner and that any future was possible. She was an ideal, a dream, and James realised in an instant that he still loved her dearly. This seemingly self evident truth hit him forcefully.

I still love her after all this time.

It was her that he loved, not the memory – of that he tried hard to be sure. This insight ended James' recollections, and again he was left with just himself.

seven

James sighed and stood up, his knees clicking as he rose. His memory trip was painful but pleasantly so. He felt more connection to the nostalgic world than he had done for months in the place that he lived, where he had seemed to just drift along in his job and home life. What had gone seemed much closer than what was now. He felt a moment of sadness with the realisation that what he could no longer touch was more real than what stood before him.

James wandered back through the streets of Cedar Falls. Walking past the arcade, he saw people lying in the darkness where they had fallen, drunken and angrily slurring their words at no one in particular. Smashed bottles and the glass from broken windows were scattered across the floor. The early hours were chilling and goose bumps speckled upon the flesh of his forearm.

A vague sound of a car alarm pierced the early morning air as James rounded the corner towards his house. He got closer to his home, and as he walked through the dark and enclosed alley that lay adjacent to his street, the louder the alarm became. He turned from the alley onto the cracked pavement of his road. Smoke wafted into the air and a faint odour of burning brushed past his nose. Though the sky was quiet, the screech of the alarm was not and as he neared his house, James was able to locate its origin.

The whine emanated from a car wrapped around a lamppost. Between the joined reams of tall yellow and orange bricked houses, the mangled machine that had once been a red Ford saloon lay crumpled on the road. The front of the car was all but destroyed, crushed inwards towards the driver's seat, and the lamppost lay bent at an ugly angle over the automobile.

A trickle of blood had run down the half open passenger side window, congealing and matting when it reached the body of the car. James paused, and slowly, his footsteps small and precise, he crept as if not to disturb some invisible yet darkly malevolent presence. He began to edge towards the howling, broken machine.

Shards of glass crunched underneath his shoes with each step.

James moved closer still and stopping right outside the vehicle, he bent forward to peer tentatively inside. A woman's head lay bowed, resting motionlessly on the steering wheel. Slowly, carefully, his right hand shaking slightly, he moved his fingers through the window, his cuffs brushing over the broken glass, towards the prostrate body. He flinched at the touch of cold flesh and choked his breath at the absence of a pulse.

James backed away. He could not call anybody. He could not notify the police or a coroner, just as no one could call assistance to aid and rescue her when it might have mattered. There was no one to help this lady, nor was there anyone to give her body the respect it deserved. She had died and there was nothing to be done.

So James looked at her for a short while, thinking that there she lay, a grisly reminder of the helpless powerlessness that was facing everyone.

Death was here, in his street. Death was at his home, at his door. And nothing could be done.

In the distance shots rippled and screams rang out.

James shuddered and hurried down the road that led home. His head was spinning and coldness spread over his body, enveloping him. He juddered the key into his door and flung it shut behind him. In the darkness of his house, he stumbled upstairs, clumsily throwing off his clothes before dropping into bed, pulling his covers tight. As he lay there perfectly still looking at the cracked ceiling above, a very real fear washed over him, and he finally began to grasp what he was sure was the truth.

I believe it. This is the end.

The chaos showed no signs of abating and in the darkness, he thought of a Yeats poem that had resonated with him since he first read it many years ago. Things fall apart, the centre cannot hold.

Things fall apart, mere anarchy is loosed upon the world. The blood dimmed tide is loosed and everywhere the ceremony of innocence is drowned. The best lack all conviction, while the worst are full of passionate intensity. And what rough beast, its hour come round at last, slouches toward Bethlehem to be born?

Outside his window, closer now, shots continued to be fired, glass continued to be broken, and he heard people's shrieks soaring across the emerging morning light. James felt his fear grow, and outside shadows shifted and lurched. He curled up closer still.

The monster is at the door, the land trespassed.

James did not understand what was going on, but some innate feeling told him that this was the end. The world had changed and the old way of life had perished. What was coming, he was unsure.

As morning broke, the first glimpses of light peeked through his blinds and the sun streamed over his sheets as it had done that morning with Danielle. James gained a measure of calm and a level approaching acceptance. If this was to be his end, he resolved to decide how he was to meet it, and these thoughts occupied him as he slowly began to fall asleep.

James had always been an avid dreamer. Each night he was carried to a realm beyond his own, one that was infinitely more varied, containing images and places he had never before seen, with rules that he could never fully understand and colours unimagined in the waking world. When he closed his eyes, he walked in worlds he created, but in places over which he had no control or choice, one that he had made but not purposefully designed. Very often it was a world that when he left he wished he could return to or somehow recreate but never could. It was a world that he wished he could remember, but he was never able to recapture beyond a vague sense of déjà-vu or indeterminate longing. As he slipped away, the many blurred images and incoherent ideas settled into one. Danielle and all the feelings that accompanied thoughts about her returned once more.

However hard it was to exist in everyday life without her, however bad some things seemed to be or how weary he felt, there was always the hope, however dim, that Danielle, she who remained quiet, distant and unseen for so many years, would suddenly sweep into view and make everything all right again. James had always dreamed that Danielle, whose heart he broke, would in her beauty and grace forgive him and bring them together again in blissful happiness. This was the natural way of things and the way that it would stay forever.

Then, seemingly as soon as he had shut his eyes, he awoke.

If this was the end, he wanted to face it with someone he was in love with. The feeling had only struck once. If this world had changed beyond any semblance of what it once was, he wanted to spend his remaining time with something he knew. James wanted the familiar amidst the strange. He wanted the simple joys of life with her.

That morning, lying in his bed, James decided that he would seek Danielle. He had always believed that one day they would get back together although he was without cause to expect such a thing or to expect that she would take him back. He sighed. It was foolhardy and self-involved to think that she pined for him, that her life had been stagnated without him. There was little prospect that she was patiently sitting waiting for his grand reappearance.

Nonetheless it was just a feeling that they would get back together someday. It was a whim, or deep impulse that had no connection to reason or logic. It was a yearning desire.

As things fell apart, James made a decisive decision. He decided to return to Little Pickering to face the end.

eight

having gotten up, James looked around his room, knowing that in all probability this would be his last proper view of it. He sifted through his belongings deciding what to take with him. He was not a hoarder, never one to keep relics from past adventures, though he did scoop up his three photo albums. He flicked one of them open at a random point and settled upon an old picture of himself as a small child of around seven or eight. He was with his mother. They looked happy and carefree. They were on a beach. He was wearing shorts and a floppy hat, and his mother had her arm around him. They both had a wide smile and all of a sudden James felt a great surge of grief and longing for her.

She was a kind lady, his mother. Selfless and caring, she was always available for an encouraging word, always ready to drive him somewhere, make him eat his greens and mind his manners. He missed his mother, but in some ways he was glad that she was not here in the confusion that the world had become. Perhaps, James mused, she would have been amongst those who disappeared. But with his mother already departed, there at least were some answers as to where she may be.

James paused for a moment in the rush of packing. He had not been back to Little Pickering since he had left. Would the cafe still be there? What about the pine trees that made up Conifer Forest? When he returned he could visit his mother's grave and lay some flowers. Maybe he could say a prayer for her and the other faithful departed. This thought offered a modicum of comfort that surprised him.

In the end, James threw only a handful of clothes – a red football shirt, a plain green top, and some spare underwear and socks – into a rucksack along with his photos and a couple of bottles of water from the fridge in the kitchen. He grasped his wallet, wondering if its contents were still relevant. From what he saw in the mall, people were just taking what they wanted, so maybe he could do so too. James put the rights and wrongs of this prospect to one side for a moment, deciding that he would probably see what others were doing. Clutching his iPod but leaving his cell phone, he collected all the money that he had, which was a figure over three hundred dollars given that he had withdrawn enough to pay his gas bill in cash at the post office and perhaps also buy a couple of books from town.

He took one final look at his room. There were stacks of books on all matter of subjects. They were his vehicle into another world. Now he felt as if he was already in one, but still he felt remorse at leaving such a feast behind. Maybe someone would find them useful one day.

A terrible thought struck him in that early hour.

What if the last book has already been written? What if nothing will ever be new again? Maybe every world has already been created and every thought already shared. Maybe we are condemned to the perpetual recycling of old images. Maybe novelty is dead. Maybe I will never experience something for the first time again.

James looked at all of his old books. Gazing at the wonderful worlds man had imagined, he felt nostalgic for the hours that they had given and the places they had taken him. Part of him wanted to take them along.

But he left them behind along with his computer, his expansive television, and his framed poster of a misty lake that adorned his living room.

Nonetheless, James left with hope and a sense of renewed vigour. Dawn had brought a fresh purpose and he found excitement in the early light. The morning sun was streaking out and he pulled up his rucksack to his shoulders and moved towards the door.

James paused. He had not planned anything in great detail and a doubt crept into his mind. Little Pickering was around six hundred miles east, and he had no transport.

How will I get there?

James decided to answer this theoretical question with the practice of walking out the door, and he set about resolving the issue with a walk towards town.

It was early when he left. The breeze was bracing and the temperature was low beneath a dull grey sky as the sun hid from sight.

James walked down his street and decided to take the main road route to town. The long straight road that passed beside where James lived dissected the centre of Cedar Falls, and he turned left at the end of the street. Though he felt a pang of sadness at his departure, he did not look back, and for the final time he left the street that he had lived in and that he called home.

Had lived in, James thought as he walked, *not does live in*.

Bushy trees of leafy green lined the main road on each side planted on trimmed lawns whose neglect was only just becoming evident. Terraced houses were packed tightly – three storeys of sand-coloured bricks and long chimneys nudged the skies.

James' watch ticked 7:30 a.m. This time last week, cars on the road sat bumper to bumper, each edging slowly to work. That day battered cars sprinkled the road, broken, smashed, and facing at all kinds of angles. He continued his walk, keeping his head down, trying to avoid taking too much more of the scene in as he battled to preserve a different image of Cedar Falls in his mind than the one that he was walking in.

But reality was destined to win out, as he saw speckles of blood that had pooled upon the pavement, first in small drips and then leading up to crimson puddles. Shards of glass lay on the road as James turned from the road onto another path. The walk to town was a trip of less than three miles through a mainly residential route.

James still kept his head down. As he came to the outskirts of town, beyond the rows of single storey houses with empty porches of lonely swinging benches, he passed over a crossroads that took him into the commercial heartbeat of Cedar Falls. A man lay slumped against a tall white building with flaky paintwork. Its neon sign, proclaiming WAIN BRO'S COAL, hung from a dark and dusty wall. The man was still and James passed him by hurriedly.

James stepped onto the flat grey space that had once a week been the Cedar Falls farmer's market and glanced around. Empty wooden slats spread across rusted copper supports on rickety structures. The stalls were coated in dust that danced in the breeze as he made his way through.

Market day was one of the things that James enjoyed most in Cedar Falls. Every week the farmers of the surrounding hills and villages would descend upon the town bringing their meats and their cheeses and their fruits. He would roam the stalls, looking at the peddled wares choosing a cut of ham or a string of salami. It was the aroma that pronounced the setting so vividly. The waft of meat on one side, the scent of fresh fruit on the other and the hustle of punters, the hawking of the farmer's produce, it was something he had not experienced anywhere else. Every Wednesday he came and each time he walked away with bundles of food.

Was this Wednesday? He stifled a laugh. *Were there even Wednesdays anymore? Did it even matter?*

James crossed the road and moved towards the largest hotel in Cedar Falls, which was one of the few modern-looking buildings in the old town. The hotel's decor had drawn complaints from the locals of the quaint town, who had considered its large curved dark tinted windows that covered the main entrance area to be gaudy and out of place. A person did not even have to mention that the hotel was the only high-rise building in the county to agitate anger, particularly amongst the elder members of the town. These were gentlemen whose daddy's daddies had settled in this area, and who fretted that the modern high-rise hotel threatened the traditions that the Falls was founded upon, traditions that they considered it their duty to make sure were upheld under any circumstances.

James had settled upon the idea that he would cross the town and move toward its far side and the bridge that separated the community from the rest of the state. From there, he could check out the lay of the land and plot his escape in a more detail. Ideally he would drive, but the road on the bridge might be blocked. If that was the case, then Cedar Falls was effectively cut off from the outside world. He would then need to abseil the chalky cliff face to the ravine beneath, where he would have to navigate the deep, cool water before scaling the cliff on the other side. There was no other way out and he would be imprisoned here.

Cedar Falls was a town where there was one way in and just one road out. Isolation was the precise purpose of the town's location. It was created as a bastion against the profanity of the modern world, a place where decent people could live uncontaminated from the moral pollution that had engulfed the rest of the nation.

If the five hundred yards or so of the bridge was blocked, which judging by the car littered state of the roads James had already passed was a real possibility, then he had a problem. He could go on foot, but the nearest town to the Falls was over twenty miles away upwards through the winding mountain road between the pine forest. Maybe a bike, or better a scooter, would be able to pass.

The six hundred or so miles to Little Pickering would not pass quickly on a scooter, but getting out of the town was his first priority. He continued through the centre of town and made a right at the third intersection of the high street. The path that he had chosen was narrow and descended on a slight incline. The stores off the beaten track of the main street lacked the slick window displays and illuminated signs of the franchise shops. But James had always preferred these outlets. Something about the swinging hand painted signs and crooked roofs always seemed richer somehow. The musty smell, lack of grandiose mission statement, and absence of relentless staff catchphrases pleased him more than the blandness of *Starbucks* and the like.

He passed a haberdashery with a crisscrossed knitting needle displayed upon the window before he arrived at a bookstore. First things first, James asserted. He needed a map. He had frequented *Play It Again Sam* since he had moved to the town. The bookstore was owned and run by a genial fellow in his mid-fifties called Ray. His store sold used books with shelf after shelf stacked with mostly hard backed tomes. Ray kept a selection of leather-bound books in a glass case behind the counter. They were coloured dark green with a swirled pattern etched into the cover. Published in the nineteenth century, these books were diaries of an explorer who passed through the region and they were on sale for several hundred dollars. Ray had once professed to James that he was glad no one had brought them. Ray liked them, their presence and authenticity. They were something real to him, he often explained to James, they brought dreams to life. For Ray, these books were part of Cedar Falls itself, part of its make-up, its unique character. They were its proud history and heritage.

James adored the shop. Layers of dust always rimmed the shelves, and a musty smell always met the shopper as he walked in. Ray would be sitting there, his round glass perched on the end of his nose as he sat behind the counter reading, his lips moving silently as he went. The shop had no discernible organisation, which irritated many of Ray's non-regular patrons, but to James it was in part why he liked *Sam*. James rarely had a planned purchase, and the random layout had led him to many hidden gems. He found great stories and wonderful worlds in places that he would never have ordinarily dreamt of looking. When asked on his stock presentation, Ray would chuckle and say wistfully, "A book is a book. Pick one and be merry."

That day James was after a map and he knew that Ray had one. The store was dark as he approached. From somewhere in the main street there were signs that the remnant of the Falls were awakening. Distant shouts echoed down the walkway that James had just left and the now familiar sound of smashing glass was again heard.

James took the first step that led to *Sam's* door and, cupping his hands, he peered through the window. In the gloom he saw no sign of life. He nudged the door with the ball of his palm. It did not move.

James bit his lip.

Could I just take what I want? Is Ray still here?

James peered in again, agitation developing alongside impatience. He knocked and waited. There was no answer, nor sign of movement within. He breathed in deeply regretting what he was about to do. With a sharp and forceful jab, he elbowed a pane of glass on the front door of the shop. A deep crack instantly chased down from one side of the pane to the other.

James poked out the damaged glass, which fell quietly forward onto the carpet of the store. Taking care not to brush against the shards of glass that remained, he slowly moved his hand through the gap and felt for the catch of the door.

Enveloping the catch, he opened the door slightly. An overhead bell jangled softly heralding his intrusion. A rush of guilt overcame James. *Ray was a good man and he loved his shop. He did not deserve this. Doesn't deserve this. He is a good man.*

Fighting the feeling that he was somehow desecrating Ray's shop, James slipped in, opening the door only enough to slide his body in. Quickly, he shut the door, again rousing the bell above.

James turned around and particles of dust visibly hovered in the creeping morning light illuminating the gloom. There was no warmth in the shop, but it was not just that it was cold. He felt somehow that the context was wrong. He trod carefully, as if he were stepping on someone's grave, and he was unable to shake a vague feeling of unease. His heartbeat quickened.

James moved slowly to the middle of the shop when he heard a noise behind him. It was a smooth ruffle of material, followed by a metallic click.

A quiet but determined voice spoke behind him, so close that James could feel a warm breath on the back of his neck. It was a breath of stale coffee and peanut butter, the tone gravelled slightly but steady.

"Get out of my shop."

Instinctively, James held his hands up, before cautiously turning around to see the person issuing the command. He looked at Ray. The shopkeeper's eyes were bloodshot, and stubble had broken out across his usually smooth features. The creases around his eyes were more pronounced then he had ever noticed, and Ray was unblinking as he pointed a small black gun at him in hands that shook slightly.

Ray looked old and tired. It was in his hunched shoulders and tatty clothes. It was in the sickly smell of sweat that came from him.

"I'm so sorry. I'll pay for the door. I just need a map. Please, Ray."

Ray regarded him for a second, before lowering his weapon. "What's the point of paying? What difference will it make?" His determination ebbed away, and Ray spoke with resignation. Shuffling as he moved, Ray's feet dragged along the carpet as he slowly walked back around the counter and sat on his spongy yellow arm chair.

James moved towards him. "I am glad you are okay, Ray. And I am sorry about the door."

Ray shot him an angry look, which then softened. "This is not okay. But don't you worry about the door, really. It was only a matter of time before someone broke in. I ventured out for the first time in a while yesterday. The mall is smashed up. People have already looted pretty much everything they can carry."

Ray leaned over the counter and moved closer to him, his words hushed. "There are dead bodies in there, James. They are still laying there. Townspeople, James. Our people. No one has helped them. We are the people to see it, after all."

"See what, Ray?"

Ray looked at James, his red eyes widening. "The end."

He looked at him in silence as Ray turned away, looking distantly at the floor, his eyes glazed over. Gently, Ray began to rock back and forth.

The silence stayed for a long time, until Ray broke it with a voice a little above a murmur. "Take your map and go. I want to be left in peace."

James moved to a long wooden bookshelf and after a moment looking and running his fingers over the uneven spines of a row of books, he pulled out a folded and moth-eaten yellow map of Cedar Falls and the surrounding area. It was well worn, but he stored it in his pocket before he moved back to the counter and glanced at Ray before talking quickly in a low voice. "I am going east, getting out of here. I am not sure what I am going into, but maybe you should come with me."

Ray shook his head sadly and spoke with a dull finality. "This is where my end is. I shall not leave my home. Take the map and go."

James moved towards the door and took a final look at the shop and at Ray before saying, "Thank you."

Ray smiled joylessly. "I wish you luck. I hope you find your own end."

A tinkle of the bell and he was outside again, feeling a hold upon his heart birthing a deep remorse within him. Ray was broken, and though he had in his own way come to terms with what had happened, he had done so in defeat.

But he is right. Cedar Falls is finished. James felt it in his heart, and he had to get out. *I have to find Danielle.*

Pulling his coat together and zipping it up, James continued to the base of the hill and turned onto a stairway that led downwards to a path beside the river, right on the edge of the business district. It was a stone path that meandered beside a face-down drop to the river on the right and was encased by a large chalky face on the left about fifteen feet beneath the main shopping area. From here, it was a simple walk about half a mile along this path of loose pebbles to the bottom of the bridge, where he would ascend the weathered steps onto the platform and leave Cedar Falls for good.

The road was rarely trodden except by those who walked dogs out of sight of the town. Sometimes transients slept down here sheltering from the cold. Occasionally couples wandered hand in hand on the secluded path, which was obscured beneath the main part of town as it wound all around the perimeter of the Falls.

He walked briskly and as he went his thoughts turned to Ray. He was unable to shake off a note of guilt. *Should I have stayed and talked it out with him? He was alone and depressed. But isn't everybody?* Like the people in the tavern, Ray had closed down. Barriers had been constructed. Like in the bar there were people together, but each of them was all alone.

Is Danielle my end? Is she just the next step? Just get to her. Just find her.

James repeated the same secure thought, a constant amidst the uncertainty. He clutched the bedraggled map tightly in his hand.

His route was clear in his mind, if daunting in the scale of its distance – left at the end of the bridge and then thirty miles to Clowes. Follow the signs towards Meredith, north-east route one sixty-five miles. From there he would be able to find his way on memory and intuition all the way to Pickering.

All the way home.

nine

James continued his walk along the lonely path. Faraway voices shouted aimlessly into the morning breeze. From somewhere close a man's scream momentarily pierced the air before the skies fell silent again.

No birds sang or even took flight on the morning James decided to leave Cedar Falls. No rain fell. The leaves on the tress did not shake or bristle and far below the walkway, the river ebbed and flowed quietly.

His footsteps crunched as they pressed onto the rough stones of the path as he moved onwards.

Before long, he came across a man who sat propped up against the side of the path, leaning against the chalky wall. His head was covered by a green baseball hat and was dropped onto his chest. The man wore grubby brown trousers and a brown jacket that did not quite match.

As James approached, the man's head jerked up.

He looked at James through narrowed red eyes and grinned a toothless smile around a creased, weather-beaten face. Thin tubes of saliva draped from his gums and he cackled at him. Hoarse bursts of laughter turned into a throaty cough as his eyes studied him. James broke his stride and looked back at the man, meeting his gaze. He froze. There was a terrible deranged madness about the laugh.

Shaking this doubt, James spoke to him with shaky words. "Are you okay?" The cackle returned, increasing in hysteria, and his eyes never left James, who spoke again. "Is there anything I can do?"

The hollowness of his words struck him. *What could I do?* The man just stared back at him, his shoulders shaking. James paused for a moment and tried to smile at the old man, who remained sitting on the floor laughing, his eyes focused on him as continued to walk onwards feeling uneasy.

Again he had met someone after the disappearances, and again James felt that he had failed somehow. He had neither found nor provided comfort. He gave no respite, forged no connection. Still he consoled himself.

When I leave here it will be better.

This was a hope that sprouted just the slightest bit when the bridge came into view.

The bridge was an engineering marvel of its day. Erected at the town's creation during the nineteenth century, the industrial magnate Henry Fletcher funded the great suspension bridge that stretched out before James that morning. Fletcher was one of the principal founders of Cedar Falls, building the town with a little assistance from a small group of likeminded businessmen. Dreaming of a secluded paradise, they designed the mountain community and cut it off from the rest of America. Sick of the rising tide of immoral immigrants in American cities, Fletcher scoured the Midwest seeking a site for a town that would be a refuge, a place that would in the darkness be 'that shining city on the hill'. In the seclusion, his grand determination was a place that was a beacon to others.

Stumbling blindly and lost through the outskirts of the Racoon Forest, Fletcher came across the great plot of land, encircled by water, that was to become Cedar Falls. In the midst of the wilderness lay this rough, untamed land and Fletcher fell in love.

This was to be his town. His refuge, his monument bequeathed to the world.

Henry Fletcher spent much of the next decade organising his ideals into a town, seeking architects and builders. Consulting reams of plans, Fletcher purchased the lumber and planned his community, damn near bankrupting himself as he went. But he never lost faith in his vision, and he paid for the bridge which he had designed by British engineer Sir Cecil Woodhead. Noted in his field, Woodhead came to what was to be the town and never left, becoming one of the Falls' first settlers. The bridge that went into the town was the last he ever designed. Simple life in the settlement was enough for Sir Cecil, as he found himself captivated within the trees and in Fletcher's vision.

The bridge took three years to build and had to be created before the first foundation for the first house in Cedar Falls was laid. After the bridge was constructed, great wooden houses were built, along with a tall white church. Crossing the bridge was seen by these founders as an act of symbolic importance where a person left behind their past life and was reborn into a life of decency and righteous innocence in the newly created Cedar Falls.

Fletcher spared no expense, and his great steel bridge stretched almost half a mile over the river below. The Chinese labourers who built it were prevented from owning property in the settlement, which quickly grew unchecked from the attention of the rest of the country. However the integrity that the Falls preserved for decades eventually started to crack as the town's magnates began to squabble amongst themselves. Each of the five principal founders of the town and their families brought up as much property as they were able and they housed whoever they could in them. Strangers began to cross the bridge, and as the nineteenth century turned into the twentieth, life in the Falls changed. Retail business grew gradually and the logging industry that dominated the town's early commerce slowly declined.

People left, people arrived. All crossed the bridge.

The bridge remained constant and unchanging, save for the renovation work of '48 and '87. But the structure, paintwork and design remained the same. It was the symbol of old Cedar Falls, when the town was more of an idea than a place to live. The magnificent bridge, its overhanging girders painted scarlet, was there before the first house and the first settler and it remained a marvel to all whose graft, labour and dream created it.

It was this bridge that James faced, and it was that which he must cross.

Beside the path he had taken was a set of stairs, the chalk steps were white and were cut out of the wall that followed the path around. The stairs were eroded smooth, its corners rounded off. The handrail leading upwards was flaky and rough, jagging across James' hand as he ran his palms over the cold metal whilst moving up the steep incline to the base of the bridge.

As he made his way up, he assessed his options. Car, scooter, or bike? In a second or two he would make that decision, hoping with each step that the bridge would be clear. Clowes was a long way off, never mind Pickering, and on foot, his journey would become an expedition that might take several days if not weeks.

With his head down, James stepped onto the level ground just in front of the bridge, took a deep breath, and closed his eyes, unsure if he wanted to know his fate.

Behind him the anguished and angry cries of the other remnants continued sporadically. Gunshots rained out, glass smashed. Cedar Falls was waking up.

James opened his eyes and looked up.

The bridge was blocked.

Cars had rammed into each other facing off at all kinds of irregular angles. Different machines had melted into a singular mass of metal, jammed compactly right across the bridge. Beyond a wreckage, some of the vehicles were nothing more than charred remains of what they once were, blackened beyond all recognition of their former purpose. In the centre of the bridge was where the main pileup was concentrated, with multiple cars tightly mangled from one side to the other. The remnants of several other cars were also strewn across the bridge on both sides, motionless and derelict.

Litter covered the road. Plastic wrappers and torn paper bags lay still in the dry air. Ripped fragments of clothes and stains of blood discoloured the grey tarmac.

But it was the smell that resonated most deeply within James and it was that odour he remembered as he later looked back at what was before him that late summer morning.

Beneath the calm but chilly blue sky, the great suspension bridge of Cedar Falls was a graveyard. Corpses decomposed, rotting in the remains of the stricken cars. The sickening smell of burnt flesh and bodies wasting away added a heavy weight to the air making each movement an effort beyond the usual exertion of simple steps.

James shuffled forward onto the platform of the bridge, wandering slowly in the middle of what was once the busiest road in the county.

The bridge was perched high into the sky hanging well over the river below with nothing but several hundred yards between the water and the steel. Behind James was the town. Before him rose a mountain with rolling fir trees that tipped the air above. To his left and right was the river that encircled the Falls, flowing a muddy copper-coloured water flanked by the rising Racoon Forest.

As James stood there alone, a wave of loneliness cascaded over him. The sky enveloped all around him, pressing him down. The air above was bereft with life, and the heavens themselves seemed to slip into an awed silence as he stood on the bridge as the sole living being on the platform. His heartbeat quickened and the tips of his fingers tingled lightly.

James moved forward coming first to the remains of a small red car rammed against the barrier of the bridge on his right-hand side. The head of a body hung at an impossible angle outside the passenger side window. The skull of the corpse was matted in a thick covering of blood.

James moved past it.

The horror of this scene was repeated again and again. The remains of a woman that had started to slowly waste away grinned through the windows at him. A blue station wagon entwined with a yellow Mini caused James to deviate from the centre of the road, as he stepped through fragments of broken glass. A body of what was once a blond girl lay face down, denting the bonnet of a black saloon car beyond a smashed windscreen. By itself, alone and isolated from the rest of the wreckage, was an empty child's car seat that lay strewn across the tarmac beside a shaggy, well-worn teddy bear.

He continued to move forward until he arrived at the centre of the bridge.

The middle of the bridge was packed tightly and it was here that was the main focus of the carnage. James viewed the boundary before him. From the left side to the right side, cars were piled together, leaving no semblance of room in between. There was no breathing space between the interwoven vehicles and they lay placed like connecting pieces of a jigsaw. Jagged cars pressed against the others, and he could tell neither where one began and another ended. He could not see from his vantage point how deep the smash went, only that it was significant.

He could not pass through.

The cars were not just a series of wrecks — they were also tombs — and it was these that James knew he had to clamber over. He looked at the smashes and then turned to gaze at the town one last time, for he would not be back, that much he knew.

I am leaving for good.

It felt strange to look at something that he knew he would never again see. *It happens all the time. People I see in the street, songs heard, movies watched, and places visited. So often things are seen only once.*

A large blue sign proclaimed a simple but joyful, **WELCOME TO CEDAR FALLS!** Typical of the town, there was no pretentious Latin motto, nor was it twinned with a distant place. There was no exhortation to enjoy oneself or stay awhile; rather, it was left to the visitor to make their own mind up.

Crossing the sign, one would see rows of houses with jagged roofs edging into the sky. A pointed church spire could be seen from somewhere within the centre of the settlement, as could the bell tower beside the town hall. To the left the hotel rose about the roofs and to the right a thicket of large fir trees could be seen. Behind all this was the hill and the tavern that stood so proudly at the summit.

Had one crossed the sign that day, they would have seen this modest town and numerous wisps of smoke rising gently within. Above the bell tower that morning, a pale sun beat down on the Falls.

James looked at all of this and wondered if he should not take a little more time. But he did not. He turned his back on the town and moved towards the blockade, pulling his rucksack close as he went. He edged close to a sturdy-looking car, broken and misshapen, its frame a chipped remains of what was once a bright yellow body.

He suppressed a lump in his throat. The window of the car James had chosen was covered in blood and the closer he came, the more he saw. His heartbeat quickened as an eyeless corpse leaned towards him, impossibly watching his every move, the glimmer of a lopsided smile creeping across his face.

His heartbeat raced stronger and quicker than ever as he reached out a trembling hand toward the car. He gripped the roof and held it until his hand stopped shaking. Breathing in deeply, he took hold with his other hand and again waited until both were steady before moving once more.

Behind him the noise of the town grew as angry shouts and anguished screams continued to lash into the morning air.

James began to pull himself up, sickened at himself.

Groaning, he hauled himself on top of the car. The roof bowed, crumpling under his weight, but it held. Steadying himself, James viewed the extent of the blockade.

It was about five mangled cars deep, with vehicles that had ploughed into each other at all angles. In all probability, he thought, they had encased bodies inside, walling them in like some kind of macabre mausoleum. Injury or the angle of the pressed together cars would have prevented many of those who had survived the crash from getting out.

They would have waited for help. They would have expected help to arrive.

His mind shifted constantly across a stream of thoughts, imaging the scene in gruesome detail.

They would have been trapped on all sides. They would have been desperate to claw out, to scrap and fight free. But there was car after car after car encasing them in. The walls would have been as unmoving. There was no way in, and there was no way out. It must have been like being buried alive. And finally, they would have screamed. They would surely have screamed for help.

James shuddered.

But no-one had come for them. These people had spent their last hours on this planet entombed in a car. It was across their crypt that James struggled, almost crawling, crouching, edging forward as he continued to cross the bridge. Occasionally moving from side to side, he made his way across, his feet twitching and moving uncertainly until finally, blessedly, he reached the other side with his heart thumping so fast it nearly beat through his chest.

He clambered down onto the cool concrete, his shaky knees buckling as he dropped. He stood and slowly, silently and sincerely, he thanked God. He was not especially religious, but he was truly thankful to God for crossing that divide.

James did not dare look behind him and viewed only the remainder of the bridge in front.

Again, a smattering of broken and mangled cars lay before him. Twisted and deformed, the vehicles were cracked, leaving orange shards of broken headlights that crunched under his feet as he passed.

Mercifully there was no further significant blockage, though this did not reduce the bile in his throat or the unsteady racing of his heart. Keeping his head down, James trudged on, looking down at his pale shadow as it crept over the blood stained road.

In and out he weaved, slowly and purposefully, he moved until the end was in sight. The base of the road moved one way, curving off to the left before chasing steeply upward through the incline of the pine trees of Racoon Forest.

With every step the scent of the pines wafted a little further into his nostrils and the noise from the bristles of the needles brushing together in the breeze became gradually clearer.

The wind was slight, the birds dormant and the sun weak, and James was close. The only sound near to him was the gentle pressing of his footsteps, and then, almost without noticing, he stepped off the bridge.

James descended the slight ramp of the bridge, and finally he was clear of Cedar Falls. He paused, feeling an unexpected but not unpleasant weight in his stomach. Again the feeling of nervous excitement crept over him, and he breathed a little heavily.

The road along the pathway through the forest was generally open. He glanced to the side of him and saw the battered remains of a four-wheel drive. A burned track of a wheel imprinted on the tarmac led to the vehicle. It was on the wrong side of the road, and its front was crumpled, its windscreen shattered. The exhaust pipe lay by itself against the floor.

James' hope rose. Attached upon the back, securely roped onto the roof of the four-by-four, was a bicycle. Taking the ropes in his hand, James smoothly rolled the threads across his fingers, nimbly moving it this way and that until it was loose. He lifted the bike slightly and placed it on the ground. He zipped up his coat a little more and pulled the drawstrings of his rucksack tightly against his body until it strained at his upper torso. He sat on the bike, and without looking back he began to peddle. The weariness he had felt up until that moment gradually departed and he began to cycle faster as he went.

James had left Cedar Falls and begun upon the route to Clowes and ultimately Pickering. As he did so, a slight wind blustered, and the first echoes of birdsong tweeted sweetly from some hidden place close at hand.

He felt as if he had truly begun.

ten

the ride was difficult but pleasant. The incline was steep in places and the journey ahead of him promised to be long. James' calves tightened, but the sun shone pleasantly down and a warm breeze gently kissed his cheek.

Cedar Falls was a rarely visited place, especially this time of year as the summer was departing, and unsurprisingly, the roads were largely empty. He moved past the odd car, each one too broken up to drive, but he always slowed to a near halt as he moved close to them hoping in vain for some sign of life within.

The hope never turned to realisation and in the entire ride, James did not see another living person. Nor did he hear a sound, apart from the brushing of pines and the noise of the odd wild animal racing unhindered amongst the trees.

The mountain became gradually steeper, and he occasionally strained to meet the demands of the incline. The foliage around him was thick and he was unable to see much beyond the curve of the continually winding road.

In spite of the circumstances, James was enjoying the ride. Feeling an unexpected sense of exhilaration, he pressed on. The wind rushed against his face as his legs pumped, and the wheels clicked ever onwards, allowing himself a hint of a smile as he went.

He felt a sense of freedom, revelling in pushing his body beyond the creeping tiredness that had been part of his waking life since the disappearances. Maybe it had been there even before them.

When have I not been tired?

As time passed its midday point, the sun continued to look down below, its pale light emitting only a little warmth. The wind was slight, barely beyond a gentle breeze in fact, and the air was crisp. Coming from Maine, James was used to far colder temperatures and the slightly bracing climate was pleasant to him.

After riding for several hours, he determined to look for a place to stop for rest and sustenance, content in the steady progress that he was making. After a while, the road levelled slightly and he came across an inexplicably placed bench that sat at the source of a small patch of trodden grass. The carefully tendered turf rolled out between the trees and led around an area of about ten square yards, which the seat was placed upon. The bench, like the grass, was well tended and carefully looked after. The paintwork was a constant, smooth brushed brown, a slightly lighter shade than the trunks that surrounded it.

James' bike crunched to a halt just before the clearing. Groaning, he dismounted. Carefully he laid his mount down onto the ground upon the road.

After the cold, hard concrete of the bridge and the coarse peddles of the bike, the grass felt uncommonly soft beneath his feet as he took off his shoes and walked upon it. He ambled slowly, as if wandering across a new carpet, his footsteps careful. Glancing around him, James sat down and pulled the water of the bag and began to drink, the cool water refreshing him.

The tall pines obscured the light of the early afternoon sun. Thin beams of sunlight pierced through the trees, spearing diagonally down towards the ground. The same scent of freshly trimmed grass that filled his nose on that day in the park an entire age ago wafted towards him again, this time mixed with a rich musky scent of pine.

He glanced around again. This was a spot that someone cared about and loved. It was neat and tidy. This was not a random location but a purposeful choice. It had been chosen for a specific and no doubt special reason.

James sighed. The pine needles bristled. The sweet scent of the forest crept towards him once more. The bench was homely. Beyond the temperature, it felt warm somehow to James. The singing of the birds was low and distant. Then, from somewhere behind him, a twig snapped.

The breaking was somewhere close. He whirled around.

This noise was joined by a soft patter, regularly repeated. They were footsteps, moving gradually closer. The steps were deliberate and slow, quietly pressing down upon the ground from somewhere between the tress.

He turned to look. The steps were moving towards him, and from amidst the darkness of the many pine trees stepped a girl.

The girl seemed like James to be in her mid-twenties. Thick, wavy brown hair swept across her cheeks and down onto her shoulders. She wore a tatty denim skirt with frayed rims that reached half way between her thigh and knee. Straps of a sleeveless green top flapped around her bare shoulders. The girl's sandals clapped about her feet as she wandered towards the bench.

James watched her quietly and the girl had not appeared to see him just yet.

Finally, she came close enough for him to notice a pattern of tiny brown freckles that arched across her nose, bridging one cheek to the other. She glanced up through pale green eyes and flinched.

Her eyes widened and then, raising her left hand to her chest, the girl smiled, her cheeks flushing red.

"Hi! I'm sorry!" She said, startled.

James smiled back, sharing her embarrassment, and returned her greeting.

The girl moved closer and looked at him, still half smiling. "Mind if I sit down?"

James scrambled slightly as he moved down to one end of the bench before flustering his reply. "Of course!"

It was his turn to blush as he shifted out of the way, allowing the girl to sit on the opposite side of the seat. There they both sat for a moment, each of them quietly looking out before them at nothing in particular before the awkward silence was broken.

"Hi, I'm sorry, my name is James. It's nice to meet you. I am sorry if I scared you before."

The girl looked back at him and he noticed a thin scarlet rim beneath her eyes. Whether it was from tiredness or sadness he did not know. *Maybe it's from both.*

"Hi, I'm Kathryn. It's nice to meet you too. Don't worry about it. It's just that I haven't seen many people recently, and I come here every day. You just gave me a start is all."

"I've seen a few people back in Cedar Falls. Not many."

The girl sighed, deeply inhaling the forest air. "I live in this area. I guess we're kind of in the wilderness, really. We, my dad and I, never saw too many people anyway."

"You live close?"

Kathryn nodded, staring into space. "Just around the corner, through those trees behind us is a path and we live along that track. My family were loggers here when Cedar Falls started up and I guess they just liked the peace and quiet." A little giggle escaped her. "They would probably love it now!"

"No one has passed by here for a while then?"

Kathryn nodded again. "Now and again I have heard a few sounds of cars, but nothing much."

The conversation deadened for a while, each lost in their own musings. The silence around them continued, both of them sitting still before James looked at her for a moment before speaking softly. "Why do you come here every day, Kathryn? You don't have to tell me if you don't want to."

She rubbed her eyes and the scarlet deepened in shade a little. "Routine, I guess. Since, you know, I just come here because I don't really know what else to do, to be honest. I tidy the house and do my chores, but since my dad disappeared I have started come here more a little more often. It sounds silly, but I still make him his dinner just in case."

She looks a shade paler than before.

"It doesn't sound silly."

He looked at her again. Those green eyes looked distant, staring at some faraway world. James spoke, his voice trembling a little. "Where were you when it happened?"

Kathryn's shoulder twitched slightly. "I was walking home. I had been to the store for some milk and bread. Crusty bread, you know, the kind you dip in your soup." She paused before continuing. "I was carrying my bag. I couldn't get it to sit comfortably in my arms. I kept shifting it this way and that, carrying it for a few steps and changing hands. Anyway, I was walking on the track that leads past the few houses that are close to us. John Nicholls, my dad's friend, probably his only friend, was carrying some firewood. It was warm and he was carrying firewood." Kathryn smiled to herself before continuing. "John had this fixation that this winter, always this next winter, would be colder than any other. I was saying hi to him and he just vanished right there in front of me, and the wood he was carrying dropped to the floor. They rolled towards me."

Kathryn tailed off.

He looked at her and she continued.

"Obviously I did not believe my eyes. I hitched the bag up and said to myself, 'Kathy, get yourself home. There's no time for dawdling.' I hurried home and put away the shopping and swept the kitchen floor. It was dusty. I shook the dustpan outside the house and sat down to wait for Dad. He missed his dinnertime. He never misses his dinnertime and then it got dark and he still was not back. I tried to call my uncle – he lives in Clowes – but the phone would not work."

"No. The phones did not work in Cedar Falls either."

"Well, I waited and waited and still nothing. It took me that long to accept the truth of what I saw and to accept that my dad was gone."

She smiled sadly and looked at James.

"What did you do after?"

"What could I do? I did the same things I did before. Tried to keep the house nice. I continued to tend this spot because this was my mother's favourite place and we kept it as a little memorial to her. She liked it. Despite how much she liked the peace of where we lived, this spot reminded her that she was still part of the world. She would come here for a while and see the road and the people that went by. So when I was lonely, I came here sometimes too, and I did after, you know, what happened. Does that make sense?"

His reply was hushed. "It does."

"But what is there to do? Sometimes I hear people late at night and I think of going to them. But I get scared. I have heard gunshots and shouting. The other day I finally got the courage to talk to someone. They were sitting here too."

Kathryn cast a glance at the seat where they sat and bit her bottom lip.

"It was a man, the day after it happened. He sat here and I came and sat beside him. He had been drinking, and his eyes were bloodshot. You could smell the liquor, you know? He was upset and babbled at me. I could not understand him. He scared me a little, and then he started shouting."

He nodded. "I have struggled with the people I've met too."

Kathryn looked back into the space before her, the same distant look in her eyes. "I sat with him for a while, but we didn't speak much. Eventually I left him there, slumped on the bench, and wandered home. Maybe I should have stayed. Talked to him, helped him somehow. Maybe I could have asked him back to the house and given him some food. But I couldn't. I'm sorry, I didn't mean to talk at you. I haven't spoken to anyone for so long."

"It's okay. It's nice. I have not really talked to anyone either."

There was silence for a while as they sat quietly next to each other. A slight, warm breeze disturbed the pine trees behind them. Kathryn's hair ruffled in the wind and she brushed it behind her ear.

"Anyway, James, I have kind of babbled on for a while. What are you doing out here? I don't think I have seen you round this place before. It is out in the beyond for you to just be wandering on by."

James considered for a moment, staring vacantly into the distance.

Kathryn spoke again. "It's okay. None of my business really. I didn't mean to pry."

He turned and looked at her. "I'm sorry, Kathryn. I didn't mean to be rude. If I explained it to you, I, well, I am not really sure I can explain it to myself. I have a load of ideas and threads of thought, but I can't really tie them together into a real picture if you see what I mean. I guess I'm babbling now!"

Kathryn smiled. "A little bit."

A tiny giggle escaped her and James smiled back involuntarily. A warm gust blanketed his face for the merest moment before passing on. He tried to begin speaking again but got no further than an incoherent syllable. Eventually, to Kathryn's increasing amusement, he got out a question in hurried tone.

"What's the worst thing for you, Kathryn, the worst part since the disappearances, I mean?"

Kathryn pursed her lips together and frowned, wrinkling her nose in a way that brought the sparsely place freckles closer.

"Well there's the uncertainty but it's not just that, it's also the boredom. The utter monotony. The mind-numbing, spirit crushing tedium of it. Having absolutely no idea what to do, so doing nothing. That's the worst for me, I guess."

James nodded enthusiastically. "That's what I thought. The truth is I just don't know what to do or where to go, or even what to say to anybody."

Kathryn looked at him and slowly nodded. "Yeah. The fact that you don't know anything. Like there was some connection between people that has been cut and we don't know how to fix it."

"Exactly. I feel as if I have been cut adrift."

"Yeah, I see that too. So what, you came up with a plan?"

"Kind of."

James spoke of Danielle. He did not going into any great detail, nor did he talk of his feelings or the emotion that he felt. Kathryn sat quietly and listened as he explained his story and the journey he planned, feeling foolish as he spoke. When he finished, she spoke.

"I guess that makes sense. It's a part of your life that you know. It gives you a place to go and something to find."

"I don't know if she is still here, or there I mean. Maybe the disappearances didn't hit where she lives. I know that it's not likely. Maybe she will not want to see me at all. But it is something more than this, more than sitting around doing nothing."

Kathryn looked at him for a moment through unblinking eyes. "So what now? You take the road to Clowes, then on to Pickering? It's a long way, especially on a bike. What is it, the best part of a thousand miles?"

James sighed, breathing in deeply again, tasting the rich pine and the bark of the trees. *Six hundred miles. It might as well be a thousand miles*. Once he realised the sudden truth of her statement, he felt deflated as he saw how utterly unprepared he was for it. The initial exhilaration had masked his hangover, which had belatedly started to make its presence felt, and his legs ached.

Kathryn continued, musing as if to herself. "Course the bike is no good. You will need a workable car. But the roads may be blocked. Then you would have to cross another barrier and then find another car. Who knows what shape they may be in or how long constantly changing vehicles would take. No, you will have to go another way."

James looked at her, intrigued. "Another way?"

She smiled at him. "You really are new to this area, aren't you?"

He nodded slowly wondering what was coming, feeling that pang of excitement returning.

Kathryn's smile broadened and another giggle chirped out. "You must have seen that great river underneath the bridge? You know, the long, damp thing below? It runs past Clowes. When the town was being built how do you think supplies came in? How do you think Henry Fletcher came across this place at all?"

James smiled. "I have no idea."

Kathryn's tone took a mock authoritarian pitch and she wagged he forefinger playfully in the air and shook her head. "Well, every school child in Cedar Falls knows. Sir Henry and his good ol' boys swept down the river from Clowes and saw through the pines the site of the new Eden. So they hacked half of it down and opened up some shops!"

James chuckled. "The new Eden? I guess they got close. So the river is the easiest way to Clowes. I'm not a great swimmer, to be honest. I have never been on a boat in my life, much less navigated one to another place. I am not even sure whether I would need to point the boat left or right to get going. Maybe I should stick to the tarmac, where there are clear signs."

Kathryn shook her head, laughing quietly, her body shaking. "Oh, James!" She gently chided. "Where is your spirit of adventure? What is the worst that can happen?"

He shook his head and involuntarily joined Kathryn's quiet amusement. "I am just not Captain Cook. He got eaten by cannibals, you know. That's probably the worst thing that could happen. Besides, where on earth do you get a boat nowadays?"

Kathryn's shoulders increased their shaking with her rising amusement. "Where do you get a boat? By the water! Where do you think?"

James shook his head, equally amused. "How do you pilot the thing?"

"Pilot a boat! Do you mean sail it? I can show you." Kathryn laughed before her tone took a slower, more deliberate, and altogether softer tone. "Maybe I could come with you."

At this, his laughter also slowed and he looked into Kathryn's eyes, and she looked back, barely able to meet his gaze.

James repeated Kathryn's offer, and both considered for a moment the implications of what she had said.

"Why do you want to come with me?"

Kathryn rolled her thumbs over each other in a continuing circle and looked down at her feet before answering. "I need to get out of here. I don't know about the whole world, but this part of it is dead. The world here is slipping away and I want to get out. There is nothing for me here. I am not saying I want to go with you all the way to Danielle, but I can guide you as far as Clowes."

"What will you do there?"

"From there I don't know. I'm not looking to tag onto your trip. I have, maybe did have, an uncle who lives in Clowes. If he is not there, then I will probably go out to the coast somewhere. I once went on holiday to the beach in a place called Lancaster Head. It was the only time I have ever really had a proper holiday. It is the only time that I have ever seen the sea."

"I like the sea."

"Me too. I was just a child, but I remember staring out across the water. I waded out just a little bit, into the water. It splashed around my ankles as I paddled. There was nothing out there in the blue. It was utterly desolate. The waves flowed, but there was nobody and nothing was there. The image stays with me, even now."

"That sounds like a nice memory."

"It is. It is one of my first and I can still picture it. I wandered a little further in and I could see weeds swaying beneath me under the water. That holiday was one of the happiest times of my life. I collected shells and held them to my ear. I insisted on taking dozens of them home. Sand was turning up in the car for weeks. The world was big and interesting. The ocean was so beautiful. It was a lovely, mysterious thing."

"Happy times."

"They were. It's like this time I visited my uncle and he was listening to opera. I stood on my own, enchanted by it. It was like nothing I had ever heard before or have since. To this day I have no idea what they were singing about, but I know that it was beautiful. Like the ocean, I did not understand it or know its secrets, but I knew that it was beautiful and that's enough for me."

She turned to James. "When I was a kid I knew there were so many places and so much to explore and I dreamt of seeing it all. But it didn't quite work out that way."

He smiled, wanly. "I know the feeling."

Kathryn brushed her hair from her eyes and continued. "I never left home. All those things that once seemed so important to me just slipped away little by little. A compromise here, maybe I would not go there, I told myself. Until in the end, I knew I would never really go anywhere and I pretended that leaving was not so important anymore, or that I didn't care."

James sat listening to her quietly.

"You tell yourself something for so long and things change. Looking back now, it all seems so clear. I stopped looking at the long term. Just get through the morning. See off the afternoon. Find something to fill the gap in the evening. God, there were days when I used to dread the dawn when I had to do it all again. But there were also times here when I have been happy, many times. You just have to balance the two I guess."

Kathryn stopped, her green eyes pale and distant.

James edged slightly closer to her and tentatively, he placed his hand on her warm shoulder, which broadened slightly at the touch. Kathryn stifled a sniffle but did not recoil. He slowly moved his hand down to her arm and gently stroked it for a while.

They sat in silence awhile. "I would be very grateful if you helped me to get to Clowes," James said.

Kathryn looked at him with the slightest well of a tear in her eye and smiled. Her lips trembled just a little for just a moment. The smile was weak, but it was also genuine and warm.

He smiled back. "I am glad that I met you, Kathryn."

Kathryn sniffed and stood up rapidly and smoothly. "That's that then. We can go this afternoon! There is a path that leads down to the river close to our house. Clowes is west of here. It's a fair few miles, but with a little luck we can be there by tonight."

James looked up at her and tried to bounce up as Kathryn had done. The bones in his knees cracked, and it took him a second to maintain his balance as she shuffled impatiently from foot to foot.

Kathryn smiled and spoke quickly, her tone slightly higher, almost cheerful. "Come on, come on! Let's go. You can leave the bike. It's just a short walk through the trees to the pier. I don't want to go home. It has become a cold place now."

With that, James and Kathryn together began their trip together.

eleven

James stooped to pick up his rucksack and pull on his shoes. He moved around to the grassy area on far side of the bench. He stepped aside and gave Kathryn a mock bow, inviting her to join him. She clutched the rim of her denim skirt and curtseyed in response, trying at first to look solemn but soon giving in to a rapid burst of giggling.

James glanced down at his bike and felt a pang of sadness at the desertion of the means of his escape from Cedar Falls.

Kathryn gently put her hand on his back and said softly, "Come on."

He paused for a moment before replying, "Okay. Lead the way."

Kathryn walked towards the pines, instinctively picking her route between the trees, not hesitating for even a second. She chose a route in the midst of the branches and trunks, ducking forward, adjusting her feet as she went. Leaning forward and smiling, Kathryn glanced at James, and with a wave of her hand and a nod of her head she beckoned for him to follow her.

Suddenly a doubt filled his mind. An unwanted thought washed upon him causing him to momentarily hesitate. Again he wondered if he was making the right decision. *I don't know this girl*. He bit his bottom lip. Yet he had a feeling about her that soothed his nerves.

James felt a vague kind of warmth about Kathryn. *But I have been wrong before*. So much so that he had grown mistrustful of his instincts. A lifetime of following them had led him to Cedar Falls and that quiet and lonely house. *Still, this girl is my quickest path to Clowes and ultimately to Danielle*. He chided himself for his selfishness. He was using her and he did not feel good about it.

I don't have a choice. Not really.

Tentatively, James followed her.

Kathryn was no longer visible, but from somewhere within the trees, her voice rang out clearly, once more beckoning him forward, again a cheery note in her tone.

James moved towards the trees to the point where Kathryn had entered the foliage. He placed his hand on a lumpy thin branch and the dark green needles of the pine gently prickled the back of his hand between his thumb and forefinger. The ground beneath his feet shifted from soft turf to rough and uneven roots of the many trees.

As he stepped into the wood, the slender light of the clearing dimmed considerably. Tiny jets of light jagged through the branches helping his way slightly, though he still stumbled forward half blind.

James ducked down underneath the branches and flailed out his hands to guide his way. His palms rebounded from the branches and scuffed the trunks. The further he got, the richer the smell of the pines became and the farther the odour of the grass around the bench departed from his senses, until eventually it was just a wistful memory.

Twigs crackled beneath his scarcely balanced feet, but somehow he continued to make his way forward, ducking and weaving as he went. After a short while, James heard the faintest sound. It was a slow singing from somewhere just in front of him.

The soft words floated towards him, the notes hanging gently in the air. "Oh, Sandy, the aurora is rising behind us."

James moved towards the noise, drawn to it. His head crazily filled with images of woodland imps luring him to a magic land of fairies and certain doom. He laughed at his foolishness. James tripped slightly, though he kept his balance as the song came closer, the lyrics sung with perfect clarity in a low, soulful tone.

"The pier lights, the carnival life, on the water. Love me tonight because I, I may never see you again."

For the briefest moment, the darkness enveloped the scene a little further. Then, James burst his way through the trees and onto a thin hallway of grass, neatly trimmed and inexplicably placed in the middle of the forest. The light descended onto the patch of grass, illuminating the corridor of turf that was no more than four feet wide and stretched forward for a span of around thirty yards before it gradually began to drop into places that were unknown to him.

Beside the grass-way, the trees were carefully lined up, as if they were tall sentries guarding the land. The tips of the trees swayed in the wind, though no gust reached down to where James stood looking at Kathryn, who was leaning against a tree pushing back the branches to the trunk. Her singing dropped into a quiet hum as he approached.

She smiled as she saw James surveying his surroundings.

He wandered into the centre of the grass, marvelling at the strangeness of the sight before him. "What is this place?"

She smiled again. It was a knowing smile. James was struck by the maturity that he saw in her expression. It was a distant look through pale eyes. It was not one of sadness but of a nostalgia approaching contentment. She took a deep breath, her whole body rising. She held it held there for a minute before dropping back, her bare shoulders slumping slightly.

"This is me and my mom's place. It is the last real part of her in my life. She used to bring me here when I was little. It was our secret place. She died when I was nine. I remember that I came here by myself and cried for hours when it happened."

James looked at her and asked softly. "What did she die of?"

"She had a fever. I was too young to really understand. She was in bed for a week. Dr Niklin came, but she didn't get out of bed. I sat in her room and read to her from *The Secret Garden,* which was her favourite book. We had almost finished it when my father sat me down and told me that I was now the lady of the house, because my mom had gone."

"I'm so sorry, Kathryn."

"Thank you. There are many places where I cannot feel her, but Mom has always been here amongst the trees and the grass. Whenever I was lonely I would go to the bench that I met you sitting upon and where from time to time I could see other people. But when I was sad growing up, or just needed to go somewhere alone to think, I would come here."

"It's beautiful. Where did it come from?"

"When Cedar Falls was being built, Henry Fletcher hollowed out these trees, creating this strip himself. He lived in constant fear that his wealth would be stolen. Forget the romantic notions of the town, he built the Falls to get away from people. You see, he guarded his wealth jealously, spending millions to protect millions. His home was just around the corner, and he built this path as a means of escape should he ever need to quickly take flight for whatever reason."

"He hid it well."

"He did. He concealed it within the trees, not even informing his servants of its existence. There were even rumours that those who built his house, and presumably the paths through the wood too, disappeared soon after. They certainly never lived in the Falls. Every town has its ghost stories, and when I was growing up I heard the tales of restless spirits between the trees, ghosts of Fletcher's murdered workers, killed to protect his secrets. I guess no one will ever know for sure. However, the story of the workers and this path got out eventually. The story of the path was passed to people like my family, loggers who knew how to keep a secret."

"There is more than one path?"

"There are two carefully hidden passages within the trees. One that leads to Fletcher's estate, the other to the road where my dad and I put the bench. This grass itself leads down to the river. From there we can go to Clowes."

Kathryn smiled again and James sensed that she had finished her story. It was as if she wanted to preserve the quiet dignity of the spot so he did not push her with any more questions. He could not shake the notion that his presence onto a place of such beauty and meaning for Kathryn was an intrusion, and he felt a rush of gratitude to her for allowing him onto such a hallowed spot.

He returned her smile.

Kathryn placed her hand on his shoulder for balance. Hopping from one foot to the other, she flipped her shoes from her feet, nimbly catching them before they hit the ground.

She spread her toes out onto the grass and looked at him. "Off we go then."

James nodded curtly and off they went walking slowly but purposefully along the slightly descending grass. The gentle slope of the grassy path became sharper and more slippery. The drop in the path quickly became so pronounced that they were now walking downhill.

At the base of the hill was the river that flowed around the Falls. It was a river of grey-looking water that dissected the trees, meandering into the horizon towards destinations unknown to him. Built onto the bank, stretching out from the incline of the grass, was a wooden boardwalk that reached a few feet into the river. It was cobbled together by ill fitting planks and looked old and weather beaten. Moored onto the small pier was a single long thin canoe that looked equally ancient. It was a golden brown colour, made of smooth pinewood that arched up at either end, and it was sleek and narrow. Perched inside were two paddles, slender and orange.

The water remained still and the pines stopped shaking as the wind died. The rays of sun shining through the trees dulled as the sky clouded over and a slight mist began to slowly drop. The twittering of birds, a companion since they left the bench, suddenly quietened. James shifted his feet, and the gentle crunch of the grass was for a second the loudest noise in that area of the forest.

Tentatively, he stepped on to jagged wood that creaked and bowed beneath his feet. The planks were only loosely fitted together, and the gap between them grew a little wider with each step he took. James moved towards the end of the jetty and glanced at the quietly flowing river. The water was tinged with a copper colour that made it impossible to see beneath the surface. The canoe swayed slightly to and fro with the current, its oars rat-tat-tatting against its side.

James paused and surveyed the boat. It was long and flat and thin. Two boards stretched out from the base of the canoe as a pair of makeshift seats. Pockets of water sloshed around the corners, but the wood was thick and solid. It appeared, at first glance, to be sturdy enough.

Kathryn moved beside him, placing her hand lightly upon his shoulder as she slowly crouched down and carefully stepped into the canoe, which rocked a little more furiously as she sat down on the seat closest to the front. Kathryn adjusted her position, sliding forwards and back until she settled, and when she did, she took hold of an oar. She crossed her legs and looked up at him, half smiling with her eyebrows raised expectantly, waiting for him.

James replicated Kathryn's movement and carefully, slowly, bent down and stepped into the canoe. She placed her hand onto the pier and steadied the boat as he took his position beside her. The seat was damp and he shuffled and positioned the oar disturbing the water as he placed it.

James glanced at his watch: it was early in the afternoon. The sun re-emerged from the shifting clouds to shine down upon the water splashing them in warmth. The wind remained barely over the slightest wisp and James once again felt a blossoming sense of exhilaration. The canoe rocked gently, and he breathed a little more deeply. Smoothly and nimbly, she untied the mooring of the canoe and placed the rope just in front of her on the base of the boat. The canoe swayed a little more freely still.

"Right, Clowes is twenty or so miles away. The water is still, but an unobstructed route and we will be there tonight. Are you ready?"

He looked distantly and dreamily up at the air around him. He then turned to Kathryn, smiled, and nodded. With a push and a heave, the canoe moved off from the pier and out into the river.

twelve

the water rippled as their canoe glided along the river gently separating the golden leaves that had collected upon the hitherto still surface. They had been paddling for a while and the pier was long behind them. The water was without a strong current, and Kathryn and James had ample time to gaze upon the unspoilt scenery as they passed by. The banks were substantial where the river shallowed upon mud flats. Beyond that were trees so thick that no one could have easily trodden the sparse land between them. Looking at the dense foliage and the serenity of the river, it was as if man had never existed at all. Kathryn touched his arm, and they stopped rowing to look at the shore on their right.

A small fawn was quietly drinking from the cool water. As they passed the animal, it paused and lifted its head to look with curiosity at them, his tiny brown head tilting slightly to one side. Man and animal were so close that he could see tiny yellow speckles on the fawn's face, and the large brown eyes of the animal steadily followed them as they slowly coasted past in breathless wonderment.

Most of the journey was spent in a comfortable silence, each quietly contemplating the life that they had progressed into. Occasionally, one let the other do the majority of the rowing, as their shoulders ached with the constant strain upon their torso. Occasionally they just drifted gently forwards with only the merest nudge in the right direction. But most of the time they flowed with the river in symbiotic rhythm, their oars chopping in and out of the water.

The sun began to deepen in shade to a crimson tone as it gradually descended into the hills that surrounded their journey. The boat continued to progress slowly. James had no idea how close they were to Clowes, but now and again Kathryn would break the silence by remarking upon the outline of a jagged rock or a passing bridge, and she would reassure James that they were going the right way and were getting closer.

Hours slipped quietly by and the sun gave way to the first throes of the twilight evening when they had finally paddled away enough miles to reach the boundary of the town of Clowes. Kathryn directed them to a small harbour area. Smooth planks of wood jutted out into the river, where a succession of boats, catamarans, and small yachts were moored.

The pier was deserted and she guided them to a vacant spot. Displaying again a nimble speed in her slender fingers, she quickly tied the canoe onto a thick metal pole that was placed on the wooden planks. With the canoe secure, James stood up, and the boat swayed wildly from side to side and he took a moment to find his balance. Underneath the canoe the water splashed around and that was the loudest noise on the pier that evening. Using the pole for support, he pulled himself forward, and he once again found himself on constant, unmoving ground. Turning, James knelt down and held out his hand. Kathryn took it, lightly gripping the edges of his fingers as she too stepped forward onto solid land.

The sky was a deep purple as James turned to look towards the town. Beside the pier that they stood upon was a small succession of steps. Beyond that was the beginning of a built up area, where he saw a series of similar tall dark yellow brick buildings marking a procession all the way down the road.

At the top of these houses were triangular roofs, with a tall centrally placed rectangular window at the top of the building. Behind a few of these windows, an ember glow emitted a soft orange light into the rapidly chilling evening air.

Kathryn stroked her arms and shivered slightly. He shared her discomfort. The weariness he felt earlier had evolved into a full blown tiredness that ached his bones. A deep hunger gnawed at him.

But I am here. The first step of my journey is done.

The next was clear. One night in Clowes and then farther onwards towards Pickering tomorrow. As they stood on the jetty, the full moon shone and James looked at her.

"Kathryn, I'm starving, I'm going to try to find somewhere to eat. I would really like it if you came with me, please?"

She stretched her arms out and replied. "Thank you, but I think that I will move straight on to my uncle's house." She looked at him and spoke again hesitantly. "If you wanted, you could come too, have a bite, then head on tomorrow? It's only just around the corner."

James exhaled, sighing. "I don't want to intrude on a family meeting. You go and find your uncle."

Kathryn smiled and looked at him, half yawning. "Okay, if you're sure." She sighed too. "I guess this is it then."

"I suppose it is. Thank you, Kathryn. It sounds silly, but I have almost enjoyed the trip. Thank you for guiding us here and thank you for your company. It's meant a lot to me meeting you."

They looked at each other for a while smiling in the deepening gloom, until Kathryn spoke. "It has meant a lot to me too. I wish you luck, James. I hope you find Danielle and it all works out. Have a safe trip and take care of yourself."

Together they turned towards the stairway and walked forward. The steps were a smooth marble colour and they ascended to the road above. Clasping the handrail, Kathryn moved forward, climbing the steps with James slightly behind. At the apex of the stairs was a road.

Kathryn turned to go left and James right, until after barely a step, they turned to face each other. They stood just a few feet apart for a moment. Each looked unsmilingly at the other with just a thin slither of the darkening night air between them. He put his hand on Kathryn's shoulder and she smiled. There was a hint of sadness in her smile, and he felt a genuine sense of regret.

"Good luck, Kathryn."

Kathryn nodded and they each turned their separate ways, and though James badly wanted to, he did not look back.

thirteen

James walked forward a few paces and took the first left past a large yellow building.

He found himself at the end of the end of a long, straight road. The wide roadway split large houses, identical to those James saw when he first stepped from the canoe. Again, the odd window here and there shone a dim light emanating from somewhere unseen. Down the centre of the road was a thin lawn, on top of which were street lights. A pair of circular orange orbs hung unlit either side of ornate, gothic style black poles.

James wandered a little further onto uneven cobbled stones.

The evening was moving quickly into night and the moon loomed largely over the street. Jagged shadows lent against the buildings, whose doorways remained still, undisturbed by person or nature. The buildings themselves were fairly featureless, making it difficult to distinguish one from its neighbour. They were unmarked by number or sign, and no brass plaque was screwed onto any of the fronts.

Before them was neither garden nor tree.

In the street, James was alone. No smoke from any chimney wafted into the air. There was no scent of cooking food, no smell of frying bacon or sizzling chicken. No baking lasagne or clinking of plates. No cat ran across the street, no dogs howled in the distance.

James stood and listened. He heard nothing. No shouting, no kids being called in for their supper. No cars, no laughter being shared.

Stepping forward, he was unsure of his next move. The night seemed to darken with each step and he was not halfway down the street when one by one, beginning at the light the furthest from him, the lamps suddenly illuminated with a soft thump.

He trudged down the empty street of the lonely town. *There is nobody here, no one at all.* The crunch of his own footsteps was the only sound that he heard.

He sighed. *The obvious truth is confirmed. The disappearances were not just in Cedar Falls. If I'm honest, I never really expected them to be.*

The night air chilled his skin and the tips of his fingers grew cold. He felt his hunger gnaw further away at him, and his bones grew still more weary. James felt very alone, suddenly wishing that he had not left Kathryn. With every step forward, the farther away the end of his trip seemed.

The distance is too great, my hope too unlikely.

He reached the end of the road and for no particular reason, he turned left. The cobbled streets continued, as did the stream of illuminated lamps and the bland, sandy-coloured buildings, as did the loneliness of the scene and the quietness of the town. James quickened his pace and the temperature continued to drop. The tingling cold of his fingers extended to goose bumps on the flesh of his forearms.

He wandered alone, without purpose or direction. He thought of calling out. He thought of returning the way that he had come in the hope of catching up with Kathryn. He thought of choosing a door at random and knocking upon it. He thought of knocking on all of the doors.

But he did none of these things.

Instead, James just ambled forward, silently despairing, always questioning his plan and his motives. Assessing his options and choices, he gleaned only the merest hint of satisfaction. Blind chance guided him, because he did not know the town of Clowes, never having visited before. After a while, he came across a rectangular sign with white writing over a violet background. The writing, scripted beside a dramatically swishing arrow, proclaimed, *HISTORIC CLOWES DOWNTOWN MAIN STREET.*

James followed the arrow and moved into the main street.

The street itself was long and narrow. A brick floored pedestrian area had a few trees spaced out and baskets of red flowers overflowed from pots that hung down from small, narrow stores that were lined upon each side lending to the street a fresh, sweet aroma. As the day continued its departure, a chill breeze whispered down the street in the twilight.

James gazed at the shops as he passed. An antique store contained old wooden furniture with a worn rocking chair prominently positioned in the centre of the display. A craft store displayed a giant, ornate loom with reams of red cotton racing towards the glass. On the opposite side, a fabric shop hung drapes of tasselled silk and a musty book shop stacked ancient-looking tomes with faded golden letters embossed upon battered spines, similar to the ones in Ray's store back in Cedar Falls. These were intermixed with continental European style cafes with outside seating patios of dark green tables and chairs. A couple of bars with unlit neon signs of joined up writing promised *COLD BEER* and *POOL.* A small, screwed in brass plated sign offered *FREE BEER TOMORROW.*

Tall signs listed CLOWES ATTRACTIONS on a blue background beside an intricately numbered and carefully keyed town map. Another sign pointed up at the sky directing its reader towards a VISITOR CENTER. Dotted intermittently around the main street were blue, backless benches, besides which were two dimensional figures of black silhouetted men and women made from some kind of metal, leaning mischievously this way and that, adding an almost macabre element to the otherwise empty scene. In the centre of the street were the same illuminated lamps, lighting James' way forward.

The street was utterly spotless. There was no litter or trod in chewing gum. The sky was a navy blue as James passed through. So deserted was the place, it looked as if no one had been here in a long time. Even the rustic nature of the shops and their cobwebbed windows lent an old time feel to the town. It was as if people had abandoned it an age ago. The only real evidence that anybody had resided in this town in the last few decades was a banner that stretched from one side of the street to another, announcing in ornate script, *CLOWES' BICENTENNIAL 1812–2012,* before a succession of others proclaimed, *MAIN ST. PARADE SEPTEMBER 4th* and *HAPPY 200 YEARS CLOWES!*

James moved down the street, utterly alone. However, he was around halfway down the procession of shops when he heard the first sign of the existence of other people in Clowes, as a bottle smashed and a scream was quickly muffled from somewhere in front of him. Unsure of himself, James shifted his feet more quickly, soon breaking into a tentative jog towards the direction of the sounds.

At the end of Main Street the walkway widened, leading to the summit of a short flight of stairs that were also made of the same red brick of the paved area that preceded it. At the base of the stairs was a giant white canopy that canvassed an area of carefully placed fold-up chairs, neatly positioned in rows directed towards a vast stage replete with clumsily placed speakers and a strewn microphone. Grass banks surrounded the sides of the area in front of the stage, and the arena was enclosed by large featureless buildings constructed from dull orange bricks.

By the time he reached the stairs, James was sprinting and he flew down the steps before bustling his way through the gangways between the rows and rows of chairs. His haste, and the noise that accompanied it, brought three men out from the dark shadows of the far side of the stage.

James slowed and moving across the area in front of the first row of chairs, he clambered upwards onto the stage. The three youths approached him. Two had quarter full bottles of beer held by their neck down at their side, the label peeled off, leaving just a white remnant behind. James guessed that they could not have been older than twenty or so. Each wore grubby clothes that were stained with grease with loose fitting tracksuit trousers and short T-shirts. Two were clean shaven, but the individual a step ahead of the other two sported a sparse, pencil-thin moustache and red baseball cap. His bottle free hand tensed as he cocked his head, viewing James.

Behind them, quivering in the shadows, was Kathryn. From a beam of moonlight shining across the side of the stage he shared with the three men and Kathryn, James could see the smattering of her freckles and a look of fear from her wide, pale green eyes. Those eyes were looking at him imploringly.

Loose leaves blew about their feet and James tried to look more forceful than he felt. He circled around slightly and looked at her before holding out his left hand. "Come here, Kathryn."

James spoke as if he was issuing a command and she scrambled to her feet, straightening her ruffled skirt. With a shaking hand, she tried but was unable to tuck her hair behind her ear. Edging nervously around the men, Kathryn stepped toward James, her eyes only leaving the floor once to glance at him who stared impassively at the foremost one of the three youths. She stepped behind James, her harsh breath rasping but warm on the back of his neck.

The lead man's eyes were fixed upon James, as the other two fidgeted anxiously from side to side. The stand-off continued in silence for a minute before the man spoke in a slurred but purposeful tone. "You are making a mistake, friend."

His face unblinking, James stared back holding his gaze and the tone of his voice as he replied. "I somehow doubt that."

One of the other two, his twitching movement becoming ever more agitated, blurted out hurried words. "Yeah? What are you going to do? There ain't no police. You can't call no one. There are three of us."

The first man leaned forward, and James could see a yellow colouration on his teeth and he felt the scent of stale booze and cigarettes on his breath. "No one is coming to help you, Samaritan. Just go and leave us with our lady here."

Kathryn tensed behind James, who shook his head. "She is coming with me."

The first man sneered, his lips curling. "Is that so?" With that, he flung the bottle violently to the floor and cracked his knuckles. James remained unmoved on the surface, but his heart thumped so quickly he could almost hear it. He turned to Kathryn and placed his hand on her shoulder. She flinched but stayed on the spot. James leaned in closely and moved his head towards hers. Her arms folded and still shaking gently, Kathryn leant forward, her breath caught in her throat, her nose sniffing. She allowed James to brush the hair from her face, carefully placing it as she herself had tried to do, behind her ear.

James whispered to her speaking low, soft words. "Go now. Wait for me behind the bar on the corner of Liberty. I will be there in five minutes, I promise. Don't look back, Kathryn, please."

He pulled away and Kathryn stood staring at him for a moment. Their eyes met and she stopped shaking. Then she moved off the way that James had come and she did not look back. He turned back to the man, who spoke with a calm assurance.

"That was a mistake, friend. We will find her and when we do, we will make it last."

Whilst he remained still just in front of James, the other two circled either side of him. James had never been in a fight before. He had always felt that he was fairly inoffensive, generally provoking no strong feelings in people either way. He was, he thought, a decent, plain man. Recently it was all that he could do to get people to notice him. He had been punched once during the course of a soccer match, but that was the extent of his violent experience and he had never been truly hurt. He had a few bumps and bruises like any child, but nothing really serious, nothing traumatic. But now these people were all around him. Their intention was to hurt him and, in a manner of seconds, they would be in striking distance.

James closed his eyes and the rippling wind stopped. The leaves stopped floating. The stars stopped twinkling just for that merest moment.

And then, James opened his eyes and the world resumed as he exploded. All of his anger, all of his frustration, all the hurt, all of his hate, all the disappointment of an ordinary life spilt over into a moment of profound, pure rage. With calmly controlled abandonment, James lashed out, and the outcome was brutal and fast. When it was over, barely conscious of what he had done, James viewed the effect of his actions. Within a minute it was over.

It felt as if he had not done it, though the aching in his fist attested otherwise. The memory was in his muscles and the blood on his hands, if not yet in his brain. Trying to regain a measure of control, James replayed the event in his head, unable to believe that what was in front of him was the result of his actions.

He had struck the one to his right first. James had not swung blindly or wildly. He had waited for his moment and picked his spot, landing a fierce uppercut, shattering the man's jaw instantly. Ducking and evading the attacks of the others, James had kicked with all of his might at the lead man, striking him with brute force between his legs. He then turned to the final man who, all alone, looked terrified and vulnerable. As James paused, the man ran away.

But James had not finished there.

He stood over the man that had spoken for the other two, looming over his stricken body. James lashed out with two ferocious kicks into his ribs. Amidst the screams of pain and pleas for mercy, he looked at the two prostrate bodies and realised what he had done. James was appalled at himself. The man with the shattered jaw dragged his crying friend to his feet, and he barely saw as they fled into the night.

The whole thing was over in seconds, and it took as long for James to compute his actions. He had hurt people. He had actually hurt people, and the truth hit him hard. His hands were shaking, as Kathryn's had before. They were shaking not out of fear or remorse but out of adrenaline. He was horrified at himself.

I had never believed myself capable of such things. But then, I have never been in this position before.

That was when another dreadful truth hit James. *If I was in this position again, I would react in the same way without hesitation or regret.* There was blood on the floor and on his hands. Pools of crimson, the product of his brutality, testified to the hidden nature that he had concealed even from himself.

James looked at his hands. They had stopped shaking. He turned to go and meet Kathryn.

fourteen

a fter climbing down from the stage and passing again through the rows of seats, James trudged back up the stairs and down the street, half dazed, his eyes wide. He moved towards the intersection of Main Street and Liberty and walked in the direction of the appointed meeting place with Kathryn. The bright heat of the sun that had beat down upon them as they canoed along the river had given way to the modest light of the moon and starlit heavens.

It had grown cold. James could not see Kathryn as he approached.

Has something happened to her? Has she lost her trust in me? She had no real reason to put any faith in me whatsoever. After all, it was my trip that has put her in harm's way. Perhaps it's for the best. The journey to Danielle maybe demands solitude. At least, that is, until I reached Danielle.

James was mistaken. He was not alone. Out of the shadows on the opposite side of the street, from behind one of the silhouetted figures, stepped Kathryn. She was shivering slightly in the cold, though she was trying to control it as she eyed James, who stared back unsmiling.

Her tone was constant as she spoke simply. "Thank you, James."

"It's ok. Are you all right?"

"I am unhurt if that is what you mean. How are you?"

"That's good. I'm good too, thank you."

The conversation stalled at this point, and James tried hard to think of something to say, some kind words to offer or some assurance of safety, but for all the world he could think of nothing. The more he tried, the darker the abyss in his mind became. Then, finally he spoke again annoyed at himself that he had not asked already. "Did you find your uncle?"

She shook her head. "I didn't get anywhere near his house. I was on my way when I ran into those people."

"Have you seen any other people?"

"No. Nobody. You?"

"Nothing at all, no sign of life."

They stood apart from each other, remaining still in the darkness. James again broke the silence. "Do you want me to go with you to your uncle's house? It's getting late. Who knows what else is out there."

Kathryn nodded. "I would appreciate that, thank you. I think we should get off the streets. My uncle lives in a big house on the outskirts of town. We could stay there overnight if you want to. It would be warm and we could get something to eat. It's only a couple of miles away."

"That would be nice, I think."

At Kathryn's promptings and guidance, they began to walk. Moving beyond an intersection, they came to a wide main road with two lanes on either side. A couple of cars were askew, rammed in an ugly manner into the barriers on the outside of the road in the same way they were so many miles previously in Cedar Falls. He glanced at the dark outline of the stationary cars, broken and misshapen. Kathryn crossed the road and invited him to clamber over the small grey barrier onto a grassy bank behind it.

Wild flecks of grass lay across a shaggy pathway through an ocean of ferns. The path began to ascend and after walking for a short while, they took a left over some rusty railroad tracks long redundant, taking them both on a route well off the beaten track. By this time, the streetlight was a distant memory, and they relied upon the glow of the moon and Kathryn's intuition. So well did she know this rarely trodden track, that she was able, with a gentle nudge here and a prod there, to allow James to evade the odd fallen branch or jagged stone.

Within a short time, the path took them to an old-looking bridge of loosely cobbled together stones that arched over a narrow stream. This was the only part of the slow wander that caused James to stop.

Standing still at the apex of the bridge, he looked out over the stream. The water was clear and flowed slowly with a quiet trickling that, along with the sound of ferns brushing together, was the only noise in the chilly night. He could see the reflection of the moon and the stars on the surface of the water, and for a moment, he lost his place in his story. The aroma of fresh water and the pine trees on the far side of the bridge filled his nostrils. For a moment, James inexplicably felt the peace of home.

The night was cold and vey dark, and they were in a spot without any artificial light. The ground was soft under foot. He breathed in deeply. Kathryn looked at him, lost in his thoughts, and spoke quietly. "Come on, James."

Their walk continued upon a path of trampled twigs that crackled underfoot as it wound meanderingly through huge pines similar to the ones that stood where he had first met Kathryn. The light dimmed further still, though she directed them skilfully. Eventually they came to the edge of their destination, where in the midst of the forest was a clearing. The pines continued all around, and it was evident to him that this place was well hidden from the rest of the world, again just like the place Kathryn lived with her father.

However, the concealment of the location was matched by its splendour. Two large trimmed lawns were intersected by a path of red gravelled stones that led to an enormous estate beyond. The stones crunched beneath their feet as they moved side by side down the walkway, which was lit by a dramatic procession of flaming torches that burned ferociously in the night, their flames adding a touch of warmth to their every step.

The building was vast. Never having seen one himself, James surmised that this is what a mansion must look like. It had several large gothic style windows with diamond shaped black panelling on the three floors that they covered. Ivy crept around the windows, chasing its way to a slanted roof. Attached onto the main building were long side walls that stretched to the left and the right. These walls were cream coloured and immaculately maintained. Large, ornate chimneys paired on the flat ceilings of these walls, as well as the slanted roof of the central structure. Alongside the three storeys of the middle part of the mansion, the side buildings had two levels of windows. Platforms of concrete levelled out in front of them. Pots of plants with herbs growing within were placed on some, and two hanging baskets of bright orange flowers dangled from the front porch.

The door that led to the main section of the mansion was of ebony construction, with large knockers protruding in an almost defiant manner. They were formed in the shape of two brass lions, their jaws open with a thick circular bar perched in their mouths, staring indifferently at those who stood before them. Either side of the porch stood a pair of sandstone figures of two headed dogs roaring ferociously at all who approached.

Kathryn noticed his wonderment. "Henry Fletcher was my great, great grandfather. His money lasted, if his name didn't. Henry had this place specially built while he was overseeing the creation of Cedar Falls. In fact, it was in here that he designed much of the town."

James struggled to take his eyes from the mansion. "It's amazing."

Kathryn nodded. "It's been in our family for generations. But I have not seen my uncle in over five years. He and dad had some kind of falling out, but he is a good man, a kind man. At least he was to me."

James looked at her. The descendent of the founder of Cedar Falls was his companion. No wonder she knew the area so well. The torches continued to flame behind them licking the night air. He nodded at the procession of fire. "It looks like someone is in."

Kathryn pursed her lips. "I'm not sure. Uncle always kept them lit. It kept away thieves. He was a lifelong bachelor. No maids, no servants. Few guests even. He just used to bolt up alone, reading. Uncle amassed an enormous library. The only time I saw him angry at me was when I was a child and was playing near a section of his books. He rushed over, scooped me in his arms and carried me away. I never went near them after that."

Kathryn sighed as they loitered outside the door for a moment before she continued. "This house is really big. When I was a child it was so exciting, always something amazing and new to be discovered somewhere. Uncle used to construct massive treasure hunts. He would formulate clues and riddles and hide sweets around the building and I had to solve them to get the goodies. But when I got older he began to get preoccupied with things, his mind became a little absent perhaps."

"That's sad. Was that when he fell out with your dad?"

"Yes. Whatever it was, he changed somehow and was not the same anymore, and no one would talk about it to me. He and father had a real argument. I was bringing them some tea and I heard from behind the door of his study raised voices. My uncle was pleading with my father about something – I am not sure what. I heard my name mentioned, but I rattled the tray I was carrying and two cups clinked together and they stopped talking in an instant. My father swept out and took my hand.

We went home and whenever I brought up my uncle after that, my dad just changed the subject and refused to talk about it."

"You must have missed him. I'm sorry."

"I did miss him. For years I planned to visit, not to resolve anything but just to talk to him like we used to when I sat on his knee and he would read me a story. I never did though."

He looked at her and spoke quietly. "You don't have to do this if you don't want to. We can go back and find somewhere else."

Kathryn shook her head. "There is nowhere else to go."

With that, she took one of the large, brass rings in the mouth of the lion. It was cold and heavy and produced a deep, solid thud that reverberated into the cold night air as she crashed it down onto the black door three times.

fifteen

the door was solid and the sound from the knocker was deep. The orange flowers of the hanging baskets brushed together slightly in the breeze. The torches continued to flicker, occasionally snapping and crackling in the night air.

But there was no other sound. No shifting from behind the door. No bolt turning. No latch unleashed. No light from behind a window was able to escape and illuminate the gloom.

James glanced at Kathryn, who rummaged around the inside of her jacket. A jangling sound was followed by the emergence of a small key ring with four keys hanging loosely down. "Uncle used to go out of town once every year for two weeks. Always the same time, the last week of May and the first week of June. He was nothing if not a creature of habit. But I never used to know where he would go. Just holiday somewhere, I guess. But Dad and I were his only family, even after the argument. It was not as if uncle had a lot of friends other than his books. We each had a key to keep his house tidy and fill the fridge and what not. Good thing we never gave it back, huh?"

Kathryn took the key. Its tip was modest looking. It was old, copper coloured, and jagged. However, at its rim were two large rings. Kathryn placed her middle and forefinger through the rings and slid the key into the door. After a slight struggle, it moved into place and she turned the key producing a satisfyingly loud click. The door moved towards them slightly, before she struggled to push it open.

The door was heavy and the further it shuddered open, the larger the slit of light beyond became. Eventually, the door opened wide enough for James to follow Kathryn in stepping through. Before he looked up, Kathryn pushed the door shut behind them and locked it.

James surveyed the majesty of the mansion that stood in all of its classical splendor before him. The room was dominated by a large stairway right in front of them that two thirds of the way up split into two directions before it climbed to the floor above. The banister was made from a dark brown wood, carefully carved into dramatic swirls. The carpet was a thick, luscious scarlet color, with yellow diamond shapes. Above them was a grand chandelier of crystal that draped down whose pieces clinked together with the brief draft of the open door. Consistent with its rustic furnishing, the room was illuminated by soft oil lamps of orange that hung intermittently in pairs upon the walls. The light was gently dim, but it was sufficient for James to make out some of the large oil paintings that hung upon the wall.

Each painting was bordered by a thick golden frame. To his left, one portrayed a great building. He presumed it was this mansion, standing tall in the moonlight surrounded by tall pine trees. Another portrayed a great grey lake with a small wooden shack in the centre of the water shrouded in murky fog.

To his right, another painting showed a man, his arms tied together lifted above his head with a spear piercing his side, his face hideously contorted into a noiseless scream. Beside it was a painting of a beast, a red-horned dragon roaming around a rural village with muddy streets dissecting houses with flaming straw roofs.

But the most prominent feature of the lower floor was a pair of armour clad knights, each of which stood on either side of the stairs. They were tall, larger than James. The silver armour was polished brightly, and they faced the great doorway in front of which stood James and Kathryn. The knights bowed their heads, their arms joined in front of them, clutching a thick sword that pointed upwards towards the roof. The dim light shone dully from the armour.

Dust sprinkled around this part of the mansion. It was warm in the room. It should have felt cosy, though he felt a strange feeling of unease. A vague sense of foreboding developed in him. Something about the place felt unwelcoming and uncomfortable.

There were two doors to his right and a single set of double doors to his left. The other option was the stairs. He looked at Kathryn for guidance and she looked around. "I had forgotten the size of this place. We should try the library first. That is where uncle used to spend his evenings. Then we can get something to eat."

Kathryn moved left at the base of the stairs, the lush carpet muffling her steps as she walked towards the double doors. The doors were a lighter colour brown than the banister of the staircase, more of a sandy colour though it too was made of wood. They were thick, imposing doors, with two large, curved brass door handles. Kathryn took both in her hands and pushed open the doors, which swung easily open and she stepped into the next room.

He followed her through the doorway. The room was dark and she moved her hand up and down the wall for a moment, until he heard a click as the wall mounted lights whirred into life. A similar gentle, dim illumination lit the room, and it took James a moment to focus his eyes on what was before him and Kathryn.

They found themselves in a dining area. A long flat oak table stretched almost the entire length of the room. Though it appeared well varnished, a sprinkling of dust lightly coated the wood. Perched on top of the table were a trio of candles, their tips blackened. At the end of it was a fireplace, encasing the charred remains of burnt logs. Above the hearth, two long swords crossed beneath a shield with an embossed crest of red and blue quarters. The floor was carefully polished, composed of black and white checked tiles and the walls were painted a dark red colour, adding a dramatic, even passionate, ambience to the room. Again various paintings hung down from the walls, each depicting a remote scene. There was a desert, a mountain range, waves of ice, and towers of sand.

Outside the wind rose to a gale and shook furiously at the mansion, rattling at three long, arched windows. That sound was matched by the relentless, monotonous ticking of a large grandfather clock pushed against a wall in the centre of the room. The pendulum swung to and fro and was accompanied by the clicking of their footsteps as they moved beyond the table and towards the single door on the far side of the room.

As James passed the fire, he held out his hand over it. The burnt wood still emitted the last gasps of warmth. *This was lit not long ago.* Kathryn opened the door and they moved through into a hallway.

The unadorned walls were plastered in dingy paper that was embossed in golden and blue diamond patterns. The paper was unclean and faded in places, though it still retained a hint of a recently departed grandeur. The floor was tiled in the same chequered black and white squares, and his feet tapped with every step that he took as he walked beside Kathryn. The lack of windows in the long hallway that stretched out before them gave the room a coldly remote feeling. The hallway was modestly lit by a succession of lamps hanging from the walls. A few of the bulbs were not lit, their filament extinguished.

He moved closer to Kathryn, brushing against her slightly, as if in an attempt to shield them from the gloom and the sense of foreboding that was burgeoning deep inside him.

Kathryn spoke quietly when they reached the end of the hallway and the door, seemingly sensing and sharing his unease. "This is the library. It contains books collected by many generations of my family."

She reached out her hand and after pausing for the briefest moment, she clasped the handle and pushed it down producing a satisfying click as it swung open.

From the gloom of the hallway, James and Kathryn stepped into resplendent light, and the library.

The room before them was vast. Enormous shelves covered the length and breadth of the walls and small ladders on wheels rested against the books. The ceiling was high and domed shaped with an arched pane of glass at its very apex. Four great chandeliers of crystal illuminated the room, giving it a bright glow out of keeping with the modest illumination of the rest of the house. Large dark red leather armchairs sat in each of the four corners, with a small, simple brown desk beside them. In the centre of the room was a great golden globe placed on a marble plinth.

James ran his fingers across the globe, the countries were raised slightly and felt warm beneath his touch. He spun the sphere, causing it to rotate smoothly on its axis, clicking slightly at each turn. He looked up over his head and through the window at the centre of the ceiling. Stars gleamed and twinkled above, chasing across the view in an arrowed constellation.

The library was warm. The carpet was thick and red, soft under their muffled steps. James moved toward one of the desks, which was the only part of the room that was not as precisely ordered as the rest of the library, as numerous books and parchment lay open and strewn across the surface.

He breathed in deeply and a rich musty scent of old worn paper pleasantly crept over his senses. *It's one of substance, a smell of knowledge, ancient, modern, and timeless.* He could well understand why Kathryn's uncle would spend so much time here. *What a wealth of studies this library contains! What worlds lay dormant on these shelves waiting for an intrepid explorer to rediscover and recreate them!*

But at the same time, James felt a pang of regret. He had spent many hours engrossed in reading, oblivious to the natural world outside. He had fostered emotions, built relationships, and felt through the characters of the stories he read. But none of it was real, and it seemed now to him that he had lived through others too much. He had missed many chances at making connections with people, real people, chances that he should have taken.

I have missed the boat so many times and now it may be too late.

He felt a wave of remorse.

I have hidden myself away from the world for so long. Perhaps I've forgotten how to get back into it. After all, apart from Kathryn, I've hardly bonded together with others since the disappearances. For months the only real relationships have been a series of intermittent, impersonal interactions with customers in the shop, as well as anonymous bravado in the tavern.

James felt a sensation of something approaching panic when he realised this, and a desperation at the sense of his powerlessness that accompanied his realisation that he might not get another chance to right his mistakes. After an instant it passed and he composed himself. Then he steeled himself.

I will have another chance, if I could just find Danielle, another chance at a real connection with another person, and I am certain that this time I won't let her down. If I can just find her, things would be better. Things will be okay again.

He sighed.

It has been a really long day.

James rubbed his hands over his face. He was weary and slumped down onto the chair beside the desk, causing the leather to creak under his weight. His motion upset the papers on the table and they fluttered slightly as he settled himself down. He found the chair to be comfortable if a little stiff.

Almost absentmindedly, he grasped a handful of the papers and glanced at what he had disturbed. They were reams of lined paper, ordinary and wrinkled. An off-colour white with a pale blue margin and grey lines, they were the kind that you could buy at any stationary store. He sifted through the papers, briefly scanning their content. Each page had been scribbled upon in untidy handwriting with words scrawled everywhere in a smudged black biro. Little care appeared to have been taken, and the writing seemed almost chaotic and hurried, even frenzied, with much crossed out and wildly inconsistent styles in words and content. The author was clearly in a hurry.

James returned to the top page and began to look closer at the text, gazing intently as he deciphered the handwriting. Each paper appeared to be structured around a lengthy verse that was ringed numerous times. From this focus, numerous arrows led erratically to other points. He read each piece of paper in turn, concentrating on the central phrase after finding the other writing incomprehensible and incoherent.

It did not take James long to read them, but he stayed silent for a moment after he had finished. Kathryn was still looking up and down the stacks of books, occasionally stopping at one and pulling it out and glancing at it for a while.

He watched her quietly.

Now and again she would get a look as if she was really concentrating, and she would bite her bottom lip and rock her head rhythmically from side to side as if she were listening to some secret music only she could hear. Then she would smile to herself and carry on.

"Kathryn, was your uncle religious?" James asked, his voice hanging in the thick air.

She carefully placed the book she was looking at back into the shelf and moved across the room to where James sat, perching herself on the edge of the desk beside his seat.

"More superstitious than religious, I guess. He had some faith though, I think. Why? What's that you have there?"

"It's some writing that your uncle must have done. Listen to what he wrote: 'And the angel thrust his sickle into the earth, and gathered the vine of the world, and cast it into the great winepress of the wrath of God. And the winepress was trodden without the city, and blood came out of the winepress, even unto the horse bridles, by the space of a thousand and six hundred furlongs.'"

Kathryn frowned. "That's pleasant. What is it, biblical?"

James nodded. "Revelation, I think. But it goes on, your uncle goes on. This is what is written on the next page. 'I will punish the world for their evil... I will shake the heaven and the earth.'"

She sat quietly listening, her eyes wide.

"Then this: 'Because they have sinned against the Lord; their blood will be poured out like dust, and their flesh like dung. Neither their silver nor their gold will be able to deliver them on the Day of the Lord's wrath. All the earth will be devoured in the fire of His jealousy, for He will make a complete end, indeed a terrifying one, of all the inhabitants of the earth.'"

He moved to the next page.

"It doesn't end there, listen to this one: 'The fourth beast shall be the fourth kingdom upon earth, which shall be diverse from all other kingdoms and shall devour the whole earth and shall tread it down, and break it into pieces.'"

James paused and looked at Kathryn. She sighed deeply before speaking. "Those are horrible passages. I am not particularly religious, but when I do think of God, I always think of a kindly old man looking down lovingly, helping us, not some furious creator. The problem with those apocalyptic passages is that there is no way in with them. There is no way to approach them or to identify with them. They are too distant, too abstract. They are empty words to me, I'm afraid."

James stroked his cheek, the bristles of his emerging stubble rough beneath the palm of his hand. "I agree with you. But everything your uncle wrote points to the passage he wrote down on the final page. It is not all legible, but what I can read says '… shall be caught up … in the clouds to meet the Lord in the air.'"

Those words hung silently for a moment. James did not look at Kathryn, and she was not staring back, her gaze was instead distant, her eyes bloodshot slightly.

"Come on, James. It has been an insanely long day and I'm really tired. Let's head upstairs, just to check that my uncle is not here. Then we can get some food and bed down for the night."

He smiled wearily. "Sounds good to me. Where do you want to go?"

"Up the staircase in the main room is Uncle's living quarters. His office is in there and so is his bedroom. When he was not here, chances are he would be there. All these rooms, all this space, but I think Uncle only ever really used two or three rooms."

James rose from his seat with a groan and lightly put a hand on Kathryn's shoulder. "Come on then. I am a little peckish you know. I hope he has some cheese."

With that proclamation, they moved back to the door. Before leaving, James took one last look at the library, at the globe, the stacks of books, the arched ceiling, and glass apex.

Caught up to meet the Lord in the air? Is that what had happened? What about the other passages? Were they describing what was to come? Time will tell, I guess.

James felt the warmth and tasted the rich, musty odour one final time. Then they left and made their way to the room that they had first experienced when they entered the mansion and they prepared to climb the stairs to the floor above.

sixteen

Compared to the library, the rest of the house was cold. By this time the hour was late and hunger continued to gnaw at both James and Kathryn. Outside the wind rose a few levels in ferocity and in noise, beating and whistling against the thick wooden doors. The carpet softened their steps, though any relief for their aching bones was scant as they moved past the stationary armour and began up the stairs.

The first run of steps led to a level platform area and then branched off either side with a further set of stairs climbing to the second floor. Together they made their way upwards to the landing, where James glanced around him. The splendour of the ground level was again replicated, though in a slightly more understated manner. There were no paintings on the walls, but they were adorned in the same thick, classically styled wallpaper of below. Small shelves hung from the walls with candles placed upon them, quietly flickering a dim light that added to the illumination of the chandeliers. All the candles were lit, though the wax had burned down almost to their tip.

A large gothic style window dominated one side of the upper floor directly above the entrance on the floor beneath. The reflection of the candles could be seen amidst the darkness of the night, and the moon filtered through the glass allowing jagged pale shadows to lie intermittently along the blood red carpet. On the wall to the right of the windows there were two single doors, simple and light brown in colour. Likewise, on the side to the left of the window there were also two doors, equally simple to those on the opposite side, producing a neat symmetry.

The entire scene was dominated by a dramatic set of double doors that stood directly opposite the window. The doors were dark brown in colour and a lion was intricately carved on the left side. On the right hand side of the door, also etched in great detail, was a lamb. He ran the tips of his fingers along the door, it was smooth and constant to touch. The door handle was large and resembled a blooming rose of a dim golden colour. It was cold to his touch.

Kathryn broke the silence. "If Uncle is here, he will be in there. This part of the mansion was designed to strict specification by Henry Fletcher himself. My uncle didn't really like people, something he inherited from Henry. Whilst Henry had maids and servants, there were times that he just did not want to see them, and he would bolt himself away for days at a time. That was an inclination that my uncle shared. This part of the mansion has a study, a bedroom, a bathroom, and a kitchen. It was not unusual for him to stay there for a week at a time, barely seeing anyone at all."

James laughed almost nervously. "Hell is other people, I guess."

Kathryn clasped both door handles and turned them. With a low click, the hinges creaked and the doors swung open. They stepped through into a wall of warmth and he surveyed his new surroundings. The room in which they found themselves was large and rectangular. It had no windows, though it had two light blue doors on the far side from the one they came in through. The walls were a scarlet colour, and the carpet was golden brown. Like much of the rest of the mansion, the room was only gloomily lit. The room appeared to be without electricity, and the illumination again came from flames. This time, however, the flame was more substantial than a candle. Four black towers were evenly spaced out in a square and placed on a singular orange floor tile made from pottery that broke up the otherwise consistent covering of the carpet. The towers were black metal bars curved and arched that chased around five feet upwards to a tray, on top of which was a torch that flamed in a contained ferocity.

Two big oil paintings, mounted on an ornate brass frame, hung from the walls on either side. One showed a large leafless oak tree withering in torrential rain as a lightning bolt vividly and colourfully ripped into its trunk. The other pictured a man stripped bare to the waist, his arms stretched out by his side nailed to a cross in a gruesome crucifixion. Flames licked his body, and his face was contorted in unspeakable agony. The picture was painted with such animation that it unsettled James, though he struggled for a moment to tear his eyes away from it. But when he did, he was drawn to the most prominent object in the room.

Between the four torches, directly in the middle of the room, stood a throne mounted on a platform of ebony. The great chair had an ivory frame, dull white legs and arm rests were surrounded by a golden seat adorned with swirls and patterns. The shiny gold was padded with violet felt that swept majestically around the ivory, entwining with the gold. Perched on top of the throne was a figure, his head slumped and bowed. As they moved closer they could see that it was a man who remained utterly still.

Kathryn edged past James before stopping just in front of him. She stared at the throne without moving. The torches crackled, and they both stood motionless. After a short while Kathryn's breathing became quicker and deeper. Tears streamed down her face forging a thin, clear path through the grime on her cheeks. Kathryn tried desperately to stifle her sorrow as her body shook. James pulled her close to him and took her head in his arms.

He spoke to her quietly. "Don't look at it."

Kathryn buried her head into his chest and tugged down upon his sweater. After a minute, silently she began to usher them closer to the throne. They took tiny, tentative steps towards it, Kathryn, still gripping James, her head still planted upon his chest. The flickering firelight cast dark shadows over the figure's face, but he could see clearly and Kathryn moved her head from his body to look at what was before them.

The skin upon the body's head had started to wither away and the features already had a gaunt look with his gums seemingly enlarged and the teeth exposed. The skull had suffered a trauma and a deep hole permeated the bone exposing a deep cavity at the temple. All around the wound, staining his cheek and matted upon his white tasselled shirt was a great deal of blood. Kathryn pulled further apart from James, her eyes closed, and she took a step away from him to stand alone. Trembling she stood, her arms still by her side. Taking a deep breath, she opened her eyes and looked again at the body on the throne. A hand was outstretched on one of the arm rests, his fingers wrapped around a small silver gun. She dried her eyes and stopped shaking. Kathryn stood stock still and spoke, her voice constant and unbroken.

"That was my uncle."

James looked at her carefully, before replying softly. "Let's get out of here, come on."

Kathryn looked back at him and smiled weakly, gesturing to one of the doors before speaking in a commanding tone. "We can get some food through there and then we can get some sleep. We'll leave first thing in the morning."

Kathryn walked past him and moved towards the door on the left. It was a metallic blue, simple, with four unadorned panels. She slipped her hand over the door handle and pushed it open, keeping it ajar for James to pass through. He gently put his hand on her bare arm, and she rested it there for a moment and then stepped over the threshold. She hovered for a few seconds, gazing at the back of what remained of her uncle. She then followed James through the door, closing it behind her without a word.

Moving swiftly in the darkness, Kathryn flicked a switch and overhead tube lights whirred noisily into life, illuminating the room in a fluorescent blue. The kitchen they found themselves in was relatively modest and contrasted with the majesty of the rest of the mansion. The decor of the room was mainly a dull grey, giving it a functional rather than luxurious feel. The walls were an off-colour white and were grubby, though James guessed that this was more to do with age than neglect. A large fridge stood directly opposite the door and was flanked to the right by a long, grey kitchen top. Various implements were neatly placed upon this surface. A wooden block held several knives with black handles, and two saucepans were carefully stacked beside a silver chopping board and a simple wooden bread bin. To the left of the fridge was a large sink with a huge basin and two silver-coloured taps. Beside the sink was an even surface that led to a cooker, again grey. The cooker had a main oven section, above which a small grill held four hobs on top. Beyond the oven was a table with thin metallic legs and an egg white surface. Two fold up steel chairs were unfurled and tucked carefully under the table, both facing the wall.

The lights continued to whirr and the fridge quietly rumbled. The kitchen retained some of the warmth of the previous room and the only physical discomfort James suffered was the now raging hunger that he felt. Kathryn moved forward and slid open the bread bin. There was a thick unsliced loaf inside that had barely been used and the smell of the crust invigorated him. For the merest moment the smell of the bread took him somewhere beyond the mansion, somewhere closer to home dredging up some elusive yet happy memory. But the hunger quickly regained control of his senses and he watched hopefully as Kathryn approached the fridge. Together they busily prepared some food.

Finally, they could settle for a while, satisfy their hunger and rest.

James took a seat beside Kathryn, each of them perched on the metal chairs at the table and they both began to chew on a sandwich. James had sliced the bread and Kathryn had constructed the meal from some cheese and ham that she had found in the fridge. After a minute of scrabbling around, he located a couple of glasses, and they both sipped cool water taken from the tap.

They ate in silence for a while. Although the meal repelled his hunger, it did not ward off the tiredness that he had already felt creep over him hours ago. He glanced at Kathryn. Her eyes were bloodshot and she too looked weary. Eventually it was she who broke the silence.

"That is that then."

James looked at her, feeling a desperate concern for Kathryn after all that had happened to her. He felt an almost manic urge to repel the sorrow that she had suffered and somehow make things okay for her. But all he said was "Kathryn, I am really sorry about your uncle."

"Thank you."

"What shall we do about him?"

She bowed her head for a moment, before lifting it to look at him through defiant but very weary green eyes, as she answered with a sigh. "There is nothing that we can do. We should stay here tonight and then leave in the morning. He will stay on his throne, alone."

"Are you okay?"

"I'm fine, thank you. Please don't worry. I loved my uncle, but he has dealt with this situation in his own way. We are taking our own path." Kathryn hesitated before continuing quickening her words as she went on. "There is nothing left for me here either. I would like to continue with you on our trip, on your trip, if I may. Maybe you would like some company? It's okay if you don't."

James finished his food with a final large mouthful, chewed for a moment, and smiled warmly at her, feeling a surge of hope spring inside him. "I would love some company, if you're sure."

Kathryn spoke with certainty. "I am sure. What else is there for me?"

She patted his hand and they shared a tired smile for a moment in comfortable silence before she spoke again. "There is a twin bedroom on the other side of this floor. We should stay in the same room. This house is exposed and anyone could get at it. It's not as if we can call the police if we get in trouble, you know."

James nodded. "I think you are right. It's crazy out there. It's anarchy. Some of the things I have heard... No police, no law, no order. There are no consequences anymore."

She finished her sandwich and wiped the edges of her mouth with a napkin. "Come on then."

Scraping back the chair, James stood and collected the glasses and the plates and moved to the sink. He twisted the hot tap and jets of water gurgled slowly out. In the absence of a cloth, he contented himself with rinsing the crockery, which he stacked neatly beside the sink. He turned and Kathryn stood up. He followed her to the door that they came in through and glanced at her.

"Are you sure that you're okay?"

There was no hesitation from Kathryn. Neither did she turn to meet his gaze. "I'm fine, I promise. Thank you for asking, though. I appreciate it."

Kathryn opened the door and strode over the threshold, sweeping past the throne and her uncle. James looked at the corpse. A macabre grin was his last expression, smiling knowingly as if concealing some secret knowledge, as sightless eyes seemed to follow his every step as he made his way through the room. It unsettled him and he was relieved when he left. He shared an uneasy smile with Kathryn, who was breathing deeply.

"We can stay in the room that I used to sleep in when I was a little girl. It's cosy and nice. I used to love staying here. To be honest, I cannot believe that it has been so long since I visited. I guess time just slips away sometimes."

Kathryn led them to the right and to the door farthest away from the stairs. She opened the simple wooden door and led them into a narrow corridor. The carpet was navy blue, and the wallpaper was cream coloured with a golden pattern of swirls embossed upon it. There were three doors on the left hand side and a further one at the end of the hallway directly opposite that which they had come through. The hallway was gloomy with only dim bulbs on the wall for illumination and there was scarcely room for the two of them to stand side by side. There was a dank musky smell in the room, as if no one had been through this way in years, but Kathryn stepped confidently along choosing the second door for her and James, leading them into a bedroom.

He hung back by the door as she stepped into darkness, moving intuitively. He heard a thick click, and a bedside lamp bloomed into light. The room was dominated by a single bed that was placed on the right side of the door, pushed up against the wall. A fluffy white rug lay on top of the same blue carpet as the hallway. The bed was tall and had two great white pillows and a thick matching duvet. The lamp stood on a small cabinet beside the bed and it only lit the room in a slight way illuminating a thin smattering of dust that hung still in the air. A large wardrobe filled one side of the wall and a large doll's house stood to the left of their entrance. The house was around four feet high, intricately designed with clear windows and a little chimney on top.

Kathryn moved towards it, smiling wistfully as she caressed it lovingly with her hands. "I used to love this. I played with this and my dolls for hours at a time. We had tea parties with our friends, had sleepovers. We entertained important and interesting people." She tailed off, lost in thought and memory until James spoke.

"If you take the bed, I'll sleep on the floor."

Kathryn turned from the little house. "Thank you. Wait here for me a moment."

She was gone for no more than a minute or two before she returned, struggling slightly with a large duvet and two pillows.

James took them from her and rolled them around in his arms before saying. "Thank you. This will do nicely."

"Good. I'm going to freshen up. The bathroom is the door on the end of the hall. It has a shower, I hope there is some hot water, but either way I am going to clean myself up. I will save some water for you, if you like?"

"Thank you."

She turned and walked out, sighing. He pulled the rug to the centre of the room and unfurled the duvet on top of it, placing the pillows at its head. He felt satisfied and it looked strangely comfortable to him as he allowed a glimmer of inexplicable optimism to creep over him. The room was warm.

Kathryn was right – it is cosy.

James sat down on his makeshift bed, exhausted and thinking about nothing in particular. It was as if he could not arrange his thoughts into a coherent order, but nonetheless he felt contented. It was at odds with everything else he had seen, but he felt calm and pleasant.

Presently, Kathryn returned to the room looking bleary eyed but fresh faced. Her hair still looked a little damp and she returned his weary smile with one of her own, before sitting on the bed. He stood, his knees snapping with his movement. He staggered out of the room and wandered through the hallway to wash up in the hope that he could again feel something like a human being, or at the least something clean.

The warm water of the shower refreshed him, though his tiredness remained, pressing his body down and adding weight to his steps as he sauntered back to the bedroom. Kathryn was in bed lying on her back with the covers pulled up. The lamp was still on and he quickly took off his T-shirt and jeans before scrambling underneath his duvet on the floor.

"I found a change of clothes, James, for you and me. They look the right size. I put them in the corner, beside the little house."

"That's great, thank you."

There was a click and Kathryn turned off the lamp, plunging the room into pitch darkness. They stayed silent for a while and his eyelids became heavy. But a doubt nagged at him. "I am so sorry about your uncle."

Kathryn sighed and spoke quietly in the night. "I feel like I should mourn him, but I am tired, James. I am tired of missing people, tired of not knowing what to do or where to go. Millions of people have disappeared and he took his own life. They had no choice, but he did. I am not that religious, but I believe that life is sacred. I believe that life is a precious gift. But maybe I should not be so judgmental. Many people waste their gift. I have, I think."

He responded in tones equally hushed. "I think maybe I have too. It's not like every little boy dreams of working in a shop, you know. I have not exactly changed the world."

"Maybe tomorrow will be different."

"Maybe it will."

Yawning, Kathryn moved under her covers and spoke in an almost cheery tone. "Good night, James!"

"Good night, Kathryn."

With that they both fell asleep. Outside an owl hooted and the wind gusted through the trees, nosily bristling amongst the leaves. The moon hung low and the torches along the garden path flickered. Beyond the mansion and the crushed grass path, beyond the bridge and the stream beneath, the town of Clowes was largely still with just a few pockets of people fighting and looting, running and smashing, unseen and unheard by the slumbering pair. No noise woke either of them until dawn had broken.

seventeen

The bedroom was tucked away in the belly of the house and had no window, so they had no light indicator as to the hour that they awoke. The room remained dark except for a slither of light creeping under the door as they stirred. Kathryn groaned in her slumber, and James stretched and rose with only his body's natural authority for informing them that it was morning. The air was still and the room quiet except for the odd rustling of Kathryn's legs beneath her bedcovers.

Stepping over to the miniature house, he put on the plain navy blue V-neck T-shirt that Kathryn had found for him and pulled on the faded blue jeans that accompanied them. She was right – they were a good fit. As quietly as he could manage, he slowly opened the door and headed to the bathroom. When he returned, the lamp was on and Kathryn was up, perched on her bed, fully clothed in a baggy black knee-high skirt with large white spots upon them and a white blouse that came halfway between her elbow and wrist with a frilled collar that circled around her exposed neck.

Through a yawn, Kathryn spoke, trying to flatten and straighten the knots in her hair that floated limply down over her forehead and eyes. "Morning, James!"

"Hi, Kathryn. I hope I didn't wake you. How are you feeling?"

"No, you didn't wake me, don't worry. I don't normally get this much sleep anyway. Or at least I don't think I do – I have no idea what time it is. But I feel pretty good today. So, what's the plan?"

"Well, Pickering is still six hundred or so miles away. If we get a car we should be able to run down at least half that distance today, maybe two thirds, depending on the state of the roads. We could stop somewhere in the evening and then complete the journey tomorrow. I have a map and it looks a pretty easy trip, I think. Not many changes of roads or diversions really."

"That sounds fine to me."

He paused. "Erm, Kathryn, I don't wish to sound insensitive, and I feel bad about grasping for his stuff when he is not even buried, but if your uncle has a car it would save us a lot of trouble."

Kathryn smiled. "Don't worry about it. He did have a car. It's not lightning fast, but it should do the job. Uncle never used it much. The garage is round the back of the mansion and leads out onto a country lane that we take until we get to the main road. From there we can get on the highway. Have we got time for breakfast first?"

"We have plenty of time."

Kathryn stretched out her arms above her head and replied. "If you don't mind we will use the other kitchen, the one the maids used when uncle had company. I really don't want to go back in that room. It's downstairs, but just bear with me a second."

After waiting for Kathryn to return from the bathroom, they departed the bedroom. Again they passed through the hallway, retracing their steps down the stairs to the lower floor. This time, however, they took a different route, choosing a more modest door rather than the double doors they had gone through before. Their choice this time led them around a plain-looking hallway and into a kitchen.

The downstairs kitchen was much bigger than the one that they had dined in for their supper the previous night, though it shared the same modesty in style and colour. The room contained several appliances and was clearly designed to provide food for large parties of people. This morning it catered only a simple breakfast of cereal splashed with milk, hungrily devoured with spoons clinking merrily on the edges of white bowls.

James munched his food happily. He was clean, fed, and wearing fresh clothes. His plan was progressing nicely, if quite unexpectedly. Kathryn smiled sweetly at him, as this time she took the dishes and washed them up, singing quietly to herself and swaying her hips slightly as she went.

When all was done, she ushered him back into the hallway and chose a different door for their next route. This door was markedly different than the others; it was larger with big bolts ratcheted on to chipped and rusted red metal. It was heavy, much more so than the other doors, even those which were made from thick oak. James opened it with a heave producing a low grating noise from the seldom-used hinges. The door did not open freely, and it took two or three extra shoves with his shoulder to allow them to pass through.

When they crossed the threshold, he found that they were outside in a narrow passageway. They were blocked in on either side by two large orange brickwork walls, dissected by a thin strip of miscoloured and overgrown turf laden with dandelions leading straight for about thirty yards to a wire mesh gate. Bright morning sunlight filtered down to the passage, and the ground was soft beneath their footsteps. Kathryn reached the gate first and unlatched the bolt.

Together they stepped through to a huge plot of land fully covered in luscious overgrown green grass, except for a small, simple white building with a triangular slate roof. The area was large and colourful and the sunlight glinted on the remaining dew of the grass. The scent of the turf filled his nostrils and he eagerly took it in. The mansion was behind them and the field stretched out well into the level horizon. As they approached the small building they could see that the only break in the long stretch of grass was a dirty track that originated at the structure and ended at some distant unseen destination.

Kathryn bounced ahead of James, skipping freely, and she motioned towards the building before playfully thumping his arm. "The garage. The car is inside. The sun is out, no wind. Let's get going, I have a good feeling about today. You're going to love the car, James, you really are."

Untying a thick, worn and straggled blue rope, Kathryn pulled open both painted black garage doors and disappeared from his view inside. James smiled at her enthusiasm and found himself sharing it. He moved around the side of the garage and approached the open door. There he saw Kathryn, perched in the passenger seat of the garage's sole occupant, with a huge smile beaming across her face. It was a smile that he could not help but return.

The vehicle, it seemed to James, reflected parts of the mansion. It had an almost antiquarian air with a hint of past splendour. The car had shiny black panels and a thick, prominent windshield with large wing mirrors and tall wheels. There was no roof, and steel bars protruded from the front of the car in a pentagonal shape. The seats resembled a single bench rather than two separate chairs, and they were covered in a burgundy leather colour perched high above the ground. One of the doors was open and James used a small black footstep to clamber aboard. The leather creaked under him, as he gleefully clasped hold of the large steering wheel.

"I never learnt to drive, James. I always walked everywhere, so I never bothered. I hope that it's okay that you do all of the driving. The keys should be in the ignition. Uncle never thought to lock them up. No one comes this way anyway. But this car was his pride and joy and by the Lord he used to make it shift."

James smiled and turned the key. With a substantial bang, the engine roared to life. "Right on! Are you ready, Kathryn? A few hundred miles and no radio. Good thing it is sunny out!"

"There's probably no radio broadcast anyway. Besides, I am an excellent conversationalist. We had better get going. Chop chop!"

With a forceful shove, he moved the stick into first gear and pressed down on the accelerator and let up the clutch. With a jolt, the car lurched forwards before settling into a rhythm moving out of the garage. The exhaust puffed clouds of grey smoke into the air as the car travelled the uneven path. The lack of suspension threw them around a little bit, but the sun from the cloudless blue sky beat down pleasantly upon the backs of their necks and the wind blew through their hair as the car picked up speed. Kathryn let out a little cheer as they began to leave behind the mansion, and for the first time since the disappearances, James felt that they were truly making process.

He shared a smile with her.

In the absence of any music from a stereo or radio, they made do with songs randomly thought up initially by Kathryn, who sporadically broke into verse every now and again This was a habit that James felt involuntarily compelled to copy, as songs he thought he had long since disregarded pushed themselves to the forefront of his mind followed by a chorus or two slipping out into the summer air, much to Kathryn's delight and amusement.

Of the two of them, it was Kathryn who threw herself into the singing, adding a sway of the head to her somewhat eager but tuneless wailing. The dusty track had led them on a straight if uneven ride for several miles past long swathes of grass. From there they moved to a stop sign and a main road that progressed quickly onto a six-lane highway. The highway was strewn on either side by wrecked vehicles. Mangled and twisted metal was entwined with the central barrier as well as laying stricken down the embankment. Judging by the number of these ruins, it had clearly been a busy time of day on this road when the disappearances had occurred.

James had to move slowly to navigate the sporadic car wrecks and the singing stopped as they drifted past. Bodies terribly mutilated were wasting away in the lingering summer heat. One window was drenched in thick, dark red blood splattered all over the glass. Another had a stream of blood crusted down from the window leading right down to the floor. The morning was pungent with the palpable stench of death hanging in the open air of the car, and though it was warm, James felt goose bumps on the bare flesh of his arm. Kathryn tugged lightly on his T-shirt as they went, trying to ignore what was too easy to see.

Though it was only a short distance travelled on the highway, this portion of the trip seemed to be hundreds of miles. By and by, the cars thinned out as they moved beyond Clowes' city limits, though more wrecks appeared intermittently on the road. Eventually they progressed beyond the sickeningly heavy smell of the dead bodies, and as they moved further away from the densely inhabited areas, the sweet odour of surrounding wheat fields floated through the air and gradually they re-found the merriment enjoyed earlier.

At one point, a car rocketed passed them on the other side of the road, and both James and Kathryn watched it with wide eyed wonderment. But as soon as they saw it, it was gone, and though they shared an almost worried glance, both began to doubt that they had actually seen it. James found himself inexplicably relieved that the car had moved on without incident. Although it was a reminder that they were not the only remnants, he found himself unable to articulate why he did not want to talk to them, whoever they were. It felt like a throwback to his time in Cedar Falls.

The lonelier I got, the less I actually wanted to see people and the more uneasy I got around them. It's a mystery.

As he mulled over this in his mind, Kathryn again broke out into song. "Leaving on a jet plane. Don't know if I'll be back again. Leaving on a jet plane. Don't know if I'll be back again. Leaving on a jet plane. Don't know anymore words."

"Isn't it, 'Leaving on a jet plane. Don't know when I'll be back again'?"

"I have no idea. Leaving on a jet plane. Don't know if I'll be back again."

James smiled and Kathryn giggled. The roads passed by and so did the songs, as they wore down the miles on the way to Pickering, crossing state and county lines as they went. The sun passed its apex and they began to think about stopping for food. Another car passed them on the opposite side of the road and this time a bare-chested man with a blue baseball cap hung out of the passenger side window and screamed as he hurled a brown beer bottle at their car. It smashed close to their front tyre, but it caused no damage. He felt his blood rush, but the incident went by so quickly and eventually relaxation and contentment returned.

"Kathryn, do you want to stop for some food?"

"I do. I bet most of the supermarkets have been looted anyway, so even if there is no one there we should be able to clean up what's left. I always wanted a free trolley dash. Still, whatever has happened, there will be a Subway open somewhere. I swear to God that I once went into a Subway at three in the morning. Crazy! I don't know why that excites me! When we get there, I'm going to make the world's best sandwich. It will have peanut butter on it. Peanut butter and cucumber."

"You can also buy bullets at three in the morning. Peanut butter and cucumber? You're a crazy lady, Kathryn, a crazy lady."

"Leaving on a jet plane. Don't know if I'll be back again."

James laughed and they rolled on by hills covered in green trees, as they continued to reduce the distance between them and Pickering. The sun began to slowly wane, although it lost none of its warm brightness, and they passed a great quarry hollowed out in the countryside. A huge swathe of trees made way for a grand drop of sandy yellow fragmented stones and jagged rocks. Large metal machinery tipped the sky, a still monument to past work.

Slowing slightly to gaze upon it, the quarry evoked nostalgic feelings within James. When he looked at it, he saw grace and dignity, though he could not reason with himself why he felt this way, and he did not speak of it to Kathryn.

There was a sadness and nobility about its still machinery. Towns would have been built around this place and lives would have been lived in tandem with its prosperity and the health of one depended on the health of the other.

But that time is over.

They passed the quarry in silent reflection and they had gone no more than half a mile when they came to a diner beside the road. It was a modest-looking establishment, slightly worn and rundown and a little grubby. Dust kicked around the row of windows that faced the road as James pulled into the empty car park at Kathryn's enthusiastic prompting. On the roof was a large white sign with ANNIE'S daubed upon it in thick red script.

He stepped out of the car and the faintest smell of frying bacon wafted towards them, dancing up his nostrils and soothing his senses. His optimism rose, as did that of Kathryn, who tugged slightly on the sleeves of his T-shirt and bumped playfully into him with a smile as they walked to the entrance. When they got to the door, a sign hung down on a chain welcoming with, HI THERE! WE'RE OPEN! written upon it. James pushed the door, which swung open freely and smoothly. They stepped inside together, accompanied by a tinkling bell.

The diner was narrow and a long counter stretched down the length of the building with red stools placed in front of it. A series of booths stood back to back beside the window, which allowed in an ample amount of bright sunlight. The seats were alternated dark blue and red with a little table in between, which held plastic bottles of ketchup and mustard, and a laminated menu was placed carefully between them. Each table was laid with a knife, fork, and spoon centred by a folded white napkin. A fan slowly whirred overhead, sweeping round, lending a pleasant, cool air to the atmosphere inside. The floor was a neat white colour which appeared to be well maintained and clean and their footsteps clapped gently upon it as they walked towards the counter.

Pulling up a stool, James sat down and took a single sheet menu in his hand. It was shiny, though it had a few stains of various colour beneath the lamination, one of which looked like a blooming flower. The menu was simplistic in content, but he looked at delightedly.

Studying it intently, he was enthused. "Oh, I could eat here! Bacon and eggs, cheeseburgers, grilled cheese and ham, thick milkshakes. Lovely!"

"Did this country's ongoing obesity epidemic pass you by then, James?"

"What are you talking about? This is proper food!"

Kathryn giggled. "Whatever you say."

"No, no, no! Not whatever! This is it, Kathryn. What, you prefer Subway? You always know what you get with them. There is no richness to them or any of the others, McDonalds, KFC, whoever. There is no context to their food, no change, no variety. There's just no character, no charm. Go anywhere and you get the same stuff, served by the same people, saying the same line. 'Want to make that a meal? Want to supersize that?' Where is the culture, where is the refinement?"

Kathryn giggled again, clambering aboard the stool next to him. "You think this place has refinement? Bacon and eggs, cheeseburger, grilled cheese, milkshakes? Should I have worn a gown?"

"Yes! This is it! Grease and coffee, waitresses, ketchup. Knives and forks! You can almost smell the spirit of the place."

"Yeah okay, sure it is. Smells like an impending heart attack to me."

Kathryn's words tailed off and their chatter broke off quite abruptly when from somewhere beyond the counter, behind the large till and the neon PEPSI sign, from somewhere passed the half-full pot of brewed coffee, a toilet flushed. After exchanging a startled look, James and Kathryn turned to a thin red door beside the counter.

From behind the door, a sweet sounding whistle moved closer to where they sat. The tune came ever nearer, tunefully serenading the cool afternoon air. The music was only just out of sight and it paused right on the other side of the wall. After a moment it resumed, and then the door swung open.

Through the door came a woman, probably in her mid to late sixties, he guessed. Her hair was styled neatly with extravagant greyed curls, and she moved slowly with a little awkwardness as she walked towards the counter with clopped footsteps.

She picked up her head and looked at where they sat, gazing in silent wonderment through round glasses. When their stares met, she immediately broke into a wide smile, her eyes sparkling, lighting up her whole face.

She flustered over to them, still smiling, and put her hands on both James and Kathryn's shoulders. They both returned her smile, though it was the lady who articulated her greeting first, speaking quickly in a slightly high pitched tone, chortling to herself as she went.

"Hello! Bless you both! I wondered if anyone would come out his way again, especially since the quarry shut down and since, well you know, since what happened. But here you are! Here you are!"

"Hi! It's lovely to meet you! My name is Kathryn, and this is James."

The lady's smile broadened further at this news and she cupped Kathryn's cheeks in her hands. "Kathryn! Such a pretty girl you are!" The lady shuffled to the side and stood in front of him, her hands by her side. "Hello, James! You look thin. You must be hungry! But where are my manners? My name is Annie. Welcome to my diner."

"Hi, Annie, I like your place. You're right, I am a little hungry." James too felt swept away by her welcome.

"Oh, I will fix you up! Fix you both up. What will it be? I have pretty much everything left. Worse luck, I had a delivery just before, you know." Annie's tone was still cheery, though she dropped her voice into a whisper when she spoke of 'you know'.

"I would love a cheeseburger. Sit down though, Annie, please. I can make it."

"Oh, James, thank you dearie, but this is my diner. I have served people here for over thirty years. I am still going yet!"

"I am sorry, I did not mean to insult you. Can I help at all?"

"Don't trouble yourself, but it's real sweet of you to offer. Please indulge me. I love my work. I run this place myself. This is all my business and I did not even let my Ronnie help me. What do you want, honey?"

Kathryn ordered and Annie swept away, moving with a speed that belied her advanced years. She continued to merrily chuckle away to herself as she disappeared back to the kitchen.

After a while, the red door again swung open and Annie waltzed through, nimbly carrying two plates adeptly placed on the palms of her hands. She put down a cheeseburger in front of James and a toasted sandwich before Kathryn to match the milkshakes Annie had brought moments earlier, which they sucked eagerly through stripy coloured straws. Both meals had a side of salad comprised of thick wedges of cucumber, sliced tomato, and sheaths of lettuce. Their dinner was met with hungry glares and after thanking Annie, they began to devour the food.

Busying herself behind the counter, Annie let them eat. They did so slowly, savouring the atmosphere, the food, and the company. As they nearly finished, Annie leant over the counter and enquired after what she had made. "So, how is the food?"

Kathryn replied first. "Just great, thanks!"

"Where are you folks off to? I can tell from your accents that you ain't from around here."

Finishing his mouthful, James answered. "We are heading for Pickering."

"Pickering, Maine? What's there, sweetheart?"

"We are not sure yet. I hope to find an old friend."

"I guess you know best. It has been a funny time since, you know."

Finishing her food, Kathryn wiped her mouth and screwed up her napkin and placed it in the centre of the plate. "Did you lose anyone, Annie?"

Annie sighed and took off her glasses. For the first time the light in her eyes died, though just by a shade. "Sure, I saw people go. Sitting right over there they were. But it is not like this place was busy, not anymore. I'm not just talking about my diner, but the area too. The quarry shut down bit by bit, gradually laying off workers, and with it the town died little by little. Shops closed, and it seemed like every other window was whitewashed. I guess folk just did not want to come down here anymore. There ain't much here, truth be told, got to go to Heaton to a drive in theatre, even further for a dance hall. I bet you folks like to dance."

Kathryn smiled at her. "We sure do. But you stayed here? Been here for thirty years, you said?"

After wiping the lenses, Annie put her glasses back on and the fire returned. "I did stay. This is my own place and ain't no one taking it off me. Lord knows the bank tried in the 80s, but this is mine, my own piece of the sun you might say. I don't know why those folk disappeared. I don't know if it was an act of God or a damn Commie weapon, but they could not take me from this place."

Kathryn put her hand on top of Annie's. "Would it be pointless to ask you to come with us?"

"It sure would sweetheart. But bless you for asking. This is my home. This is all I know and all I want. It may sound sad, probably some them city types would call it small town thinking. Maybe I have not made something of my life in the way the movies talk about things, but I have spent my life happy. That is enough for me, and I know that I have been blessed, uncommonly so, I think"

James smiled sadly. "Few people achieve that, I think. I wish I had."

"You still can do honey. You ain't done yet. Maybe you will find it in Pickering. I sure hope so. You both seem like such nice kids. This place has always been here for me, sharing my happiness and sadness. It has here that I spent such moments and shared as others experienced their own. Serving food, pouring coffee, to me this is the world. Whether people are here or not, this diner is like a living thing to me. I can't leave her be. I have never really known what was going on in the world and this time it is no different, but whatever – you just try to make the best of things. You just get on with it, don't you?"

Annie paused and then looked again at Kathryn before saying hurriedly. "Now now, don't I feel like the chatterbox! I don't normally talk so much, that I can promise you! I usually just sit back and listen to the folks. Kind of a role reversal today!"

James looked at her. "It has been nice to listen to, Annie."

Annie breathed in deeply. "Have you guys had enough? It's a long way to Pickering. You'll want to be getting off soon, I guess. You know where you are heading? It is a real easy ride from here."

Kathryn glanced at James and then back at Annie. "We are in no rush. Are we, James?"

"Not at all."

Annie splashed some coffee in a pair of white ceramic cups and placed one each in front of them. James spoke again. "Why don't you join us? Have a drink with us, please?"

Annie smiled. "No time, sweetheart. I am cleaning the kitchen, then I got to do a stock take, then clean the windows. Lots to do, always lots to do."

Kathryn looked at her imploringly, her tone faltering. "Please, is there any job we can do, anything that we can do to help?"

Annie laughed a throaty laugh and slapped Kathryn's arm playfully. "Ain't you been listening, sweetheart? This is my place, bless you! You don't need to worry about me. I have everything here I want."

Kathryn looked at her. "Thank you, Annie. I have really enjoyed my food and talking to you."

"I enjoyed mine too. Thank you."

"Well, what a lovely thing to say! I like to think I got the cooking right after so long, wouldn't be much use if I hadn't now, would I! Tell you what. For listening to me yak on and on, there ain't no charge from me today. Now, now, don't be protesting. I told you twice, this is my place and my rules. Money seems a little pointless nowadays anyway, don't it?"

James moved to talk, but Annie glared at him with a reproaching look and took his hand, squeezing it affectionately. He smiled at her. Both James and Kathryn took their time, mulling over their coffee. Annie busied herself behind the counter wiping and scrubbing away the surfaces. Though they dragged out the time leading up to their departure, none of the three of them really spoke much.

The clock ticked on and the excuses for staying gradually drifted away, though James felt a rising feeling of unease the closer he got to the end of his drink.

Eventually Annie slowly, almost apologetically, picked up the empty mugs with a smile. He felt a friendliness and warmth coming from her smile, and Pickering seemed like a distant dream at this point.

But he stood, and after hesitating, Kathryn joined him. Gently, he lifted his hand to Annie's shoulder and slowly stroked it. Annie looked at him, the same defiance undiminished in her eyes. After a short while he let go and walked away from her. Kathryn took his place and took both her hands and spoke in a wobbled tone. "Goodbye Annie. Thank you again. Bless you."

Annie smiled strongly. "You kids take care. Come again now you hear, and tell all your friends too."

James held open the jangling door for Kathryn, who walked quickly passed him with her head bowed. He took a last look at the diner, empty except for Annie, who looked back holding two cups in her right hand.

She stood smiling and nodded at him.

"Look after yourself, Annie."

"Always do, sweetheart!"

With that James walked out and shut the door behind him. He crossed the empty car park and got into the vehicle where Kathryn already sat waiting for him. The car started with another bang, and he pulled out onto the highway again, taking another step on the road to Pickering.

They drove in silence for a while. James glanced at Kathryn. Tears were welling up in her eyes matching the ache low down in his own stomach.

They drove on.

eighteen

the miles went by in silence for a long while, as the sorrow that they each felt went unspoken. For James the quiet was something of relief. Leaving behind Annie was a wretch, but it was a selfish sadness. Annie had chosen to stay behind, he had not abandoned her.

I have not abandoned her. I have not.

James repeated that in his head over and over again.

Annie wanted to remain there. It's where she belongs. Besides, what the hell could I offer her? I have only a vague plan. I am, in fact, seeking a place like Annie's. A place of security, a sense of belonging, a home to stay. That is what Annie had.

Do I regret leaving her, or it is envy at what she has?

Such questions brought yet more wonderings and fresh doubts.

Yes, I do seek the sense of belonging that Annie enjoys, but what about Kathryn? How can I provide that for her when I have not been thus far able to do so for myself? No, she deserves far more than this. She deserves what Annie has.

Annie was only the second person that he had really connected with since the disappearances. It was one meeting that had lasted only around an hour, with just a few little words in the way of conversation with a lady in a diner.

Why do I feel this way? Why do I feel sad about leaving? Maybe it was the kindness she had shown, the smiling face and pleasant words. That gave Annie grace, a grace that has been absent in my life for a long time before I met her and Kathryn.

Though he kept thinking about Annie, James eventually began to shake it off, feeling a little foolish for his emotions, though they still nagged at him. For the first time since they had got to know each other, James had felt a gap between him and Kathryn when they left the diner, but this did not last for too long, and before the afternoon made way for evening, that distance had shortened, and they began to laugh and chat again in comfort. The uneasiness lessened as the mile count from the diner increased. Slowly, they regained the ease of each other's company.

The conversation was light as the blaze of the afternoon sun dimmed. They laughed about old pets, James' goldfish and Kathryn's sock-nibbling golden retriever, and they giggled about youthful misadventures and reminisced old television shows.

The miles on the highway rolled relentlessly on by as they drove the long grey straight road forwards, never quite reaching the horizon. The scenery rarely changed, but still their spirits did not drop. The time passed by pleasantly and the weather remained fine. The glint of the sun was not as blindingly harsh as it had been when they began their journey, as its slow descent into the horizon behind them softened the warmth. They had changed highways a couple of times but progressed forward on sparse tracks occasionally dodging the odd damaged car. Again vehicles sometimes crossed them on the opposite side of the road, though apart from curious glances, none demonstrated even the slightest interest in them. Eventually, after many hours of driving, including one awkward but uneventful and free stop at an empty gas station, the trees that surrounded the road began to tip the sun and the evening deepened into a navy blue sky.

The air chilled slightly and a wisp of wind scattered over the two of them. Kathryn reached in the backseat and pulled on a black woollen cardigan and turned to James. "The day's getting on, but we have made decent time, I think. Shall we stop and bed down for the night? We can probably make Pickering at some point tomorrow."

"Good idea. I really don't know this area though. I probably should, but I have no idea. I swear to God I get lost everywhere I go. It's a miracle that we have made it this far. I lived in Pickering eighteen years and still used to get lost every now and again."

"Well, I have never been this far east in my life, we may as well be in the USSR."

"I think you mean Russia and its independent states nowadays."

"Yeah, there too. Let's just pick a place we like the sound of, like Lake Titicaca."

James giggled as they passed a sign with a series of place names and distances. "I like that name too. How about this one, Munt?"

"Munt? Sounds crude. What about this town, Mount Pleasant, fifteen miles? Sounds a little too artificially idyllic, but at least it is not Munt."

"Mount Pleasant it is."

The fifteen miles shot by smoothly. The wind picked up as they went and the temperature dropped still further. It was getting cold in the exposed car, but they quickly reached the turnoff. The dual lane highway exit curved away in a large semicircle between rows of green trees taking them across a bridge over a flowing river. The two lanes merged into one as they began the road into Mount Pleasant, carefully following the signs as they went. From the speed of the highway, it seemed to him as if the car was crawling as they slowed in the straight run into town.

After a short distance they drove beyond a sign that proclaimed *MOUNT PLEASANT – population 40,000.* The size of the town seemed at first to contradict its modest population. The buildings, though tightly congested, were of not inconsiderable size. They were nowhere near the scale of even the moderately sized cities of the east, but many were still larger than those of Cedar Falls, as numerous storeys silhouetted the darkening skyline.

The electricity persisted in Mount Pleasant, something James wondered if they could still take for granted. Nonetheless, orange streetlights illuminated their drive through the centre of town, and they made their way on instinct, choosing the route according to their own preferences and whims. Eventually they came across a large, pale marble cenotaph that pointed like the tip of an arrow towards the now navy blue sky, puncturing the moon within. On the other side of the war memorial was a tall building of many windows. A lit up blue sign protruded from the entrance catching eyes with the words *CLERMON HOTEL ****.* Beyond this sign were brown shaded doors, with the slightest embers of dim light shining from somewhere behind.

James parked the car right next to the curb and looked at the hotel. "Well, I guess we may as well stay in style. Shall we?"

"That we shall, James!"

Together, they both got out of the car, eager to get inside from the chilly early night air. They walked into the drive in archway of the hotel and moved to the tinted doors. James pushed one of the glass doors open, smearing his handprints upon it as he held it open for Kathryn to pass through.

They entered into a reception area and a wall of heat instantly wrapped around them producing a sense of comfortable warmth. The decor of the lobby was neat and tidy. A coat rack hung beside a hat stand and a bucket of black umbrellas was right next to the door. The carpet was thick and golden and cushioned their steps to a hollowed out wooden counter upon which stood a brass-coloured triangular sign reading **RECEPTION** in bold type. Behind was a series of numbered pigeon holes, a few of which had some rolled up papers and envelopes stuffed inside. Also on top of the counter was an open visitor's book that read like a ledger, with reams of names, addresses, and signatures carefully recorded alongside dates. James glanced at the book. There had been no entry since the disappearances. Kathryn sidled up to the counter and noticed a small, old-fashioned-looking bell, silver in colour with a little button on top. She tapped the button twice in rapid succession and a double ring chimed into the still air.

Barely a heartbeat went by before a man appeared behind the counter.

"Double room? One hundred and eighty dollars a night. En suite, special seasonal rates. Check out time is midday."

Looking at them through small, black beady eyes behind rimmed glasses, the man spoke in a soft nasally whine. He appeared to be in his early forties and was well groomed, with dark slicked back hair, carefully combed over a thinning crown. His pale face was lined and his nose crooked over a neatly trimmed moustache that curled upwards on either side. He wore a black suit that tightly fitted his oval shape and his outfit was rounded off with a black waistcoat, a white shirt and a scarlet bowtie. After the man finished speaking, the edges of his thin, blood red lips twitched for a moment. At the hint of a pause, the man looked expectantly at James and Kathryn with raised eyebrows.

"That is, one hundred and eighty dollars for a suite, special seasonal rate."

James repelled his surprise, snapping to attention. "Erm, okay, sounds fair enough to me. Kathryn, is that okay with you?"

"Yes, that's fine." Kathryn smiled hastily, her eyes wide.

"Excellent. Room service is off, I am afraid, but you can still get some food in town. I am also afraid that our porter is, ahem, missing this evening, but you don't seem to have any heavy bags?"

"No, no bags today," James replied.

"Good. I am Mr Aubrey, the manager of this hotel, and I am at your service for the duration of your stay here. This way please. I am putting you on the fifth floor."

The man took a door at the side of the counter and swept out into the reception, his jacket tail blustering behind him. Gesturing for them to follow, Mr Aubrey walked forward and climbed a short flight of four or five steps, guiding them to a small hallway, where two elevators with brass-coloured doors quietly awaited. Mr Aubrey pressed an arrow shaped button that pointed to the ceiling, and after a short time one of the brass doors slid smoothly open.

After ushering them inside, Mr Aubrey followed them in. The elevator was spacious and spotlessly clean, from the red carpet to the polished mirror opposite the doors, it was immaculate. A dim orange light lit their short journey upwards, until they stepped out onto the fifth floor. Taking the lead, twirling the single key nimbly on his forefinger, Mr Aubrey stopped at room 518 and slipped the key into the lock, opening the door for them. James went in first, followed by Kathryn and finally Mr Aubrey, who shut the door behind him.

The room was expansive and split into three mini rooms, which they wandered through. It contained two single beds placed side by side with a crimson duvet and two plump pillows. A lamp hung above each bed and a small table divided them, a vase of artificial-looking violet flowers hanging limply on top. This space crossed almost seamlessly into a seating area comprising of a tinted glass coffee table and a black leather sofa, beside which was a single matching armchair. A large window was concealed in this room behind dark purple curtains, velvet in appearance. The suite was lit with a soft orange light, illuminating the comfortable brown carpet.

The room was pleasantly warm.

The four stars are well justified.

"I trust this room is to your liking?" Mr Aubrey faced both of them, his hands joined together in front of him.

Kathryn answered. "Yes, thank you, Mr Aubrey. It's lovely."

"Excellent. We can deal with the paperwork presently. How long will you be staying with us?"

This time, James replied. "Just the one night. How many other people are staying tonight?"

"A few are staying with us. Not many, but a few here and there. They should not make much noise though. We don't tend to attract that kind of clientele, you understand."

Kathryn spoke again. "You said we could get some food in town, Mr Aubrey? Where would you recommend?"

Mr Aubrey paused and his brow furrowed momentarily. "I am sure I do not need to inform that in the, ahem, current climate, the options for dining are limited."

James nodded and Mr Aubrey continued.

"I am afraid that it is not an exaggeration to say that only one place remains serving food in Mount Pleasant, and the choice there is rather limited, even if the price is agreeable."

"Which place is it? I feel like I could eat a horse!" Kathryn stifled a giggle, but Mr Aubrey was unmoved as replied in the same earnest tone. His words quickened and as James listened, he detected the first sign of enthusiasm emerging beyond his evident sense of strict professionalism.

Mr Aubrey was no longer talking to just customers.

"Saint Mark's Church. You will find it on Partridge Avenue, which is just eight blocks west of here. It is a large building and many town meetings are held there. Many of those left in Mount Pleasant have gone there these past few evenings, and the pastor feeds them and discusses important matters with them. I am sure that I do not need to tell you that he has been very busy. You are in for a treat this evening. I gather the pastor has chosen tonight to give a special sermon to the town. There has been quite the buzz around the place. I understand that people are coming from quite a way to hear him. I myself am going later on when I finish up here. Perhaps I could show you the way – if that is agreeable?"

James answered. "That would be very kind, thank you – if that is okay with you, Kathryn?"

Kathryn nodded. "I guess I know what he is going to talk about, if not what he will say."

They arranged a time to meet and Mr Aubrey bowed slightly to them and then made his way out of the room, leaving them alone.

Kathryn perched on the edge of the bed, springing up and down for a moment creaking the springs in the mattress. James moved into the sitting area and turned on the television. After a moment the screen flickered to life, but it failed to settle into a picture, producing only a scrambled blur and white noise on every channel.

He switched it off and returned to the bedroom and sat on the bed next to Kathryn, letting out a weary sigh.

"What do you make of this, Kathryn, going to church, I mean?"

"Well, I've got no answers at the moment. Maybe this pastor has something, but I doubt it. Either way I am going to keep an open mind I think, if not a bated breath. It would be nice to get some food, though. My stomach is rumbling in a most unladylike way."

"I guess, but I am a little worried."

"Worried? Why?"

"People are afraid. It does not take much to turn fear into hate and anger. We have both seen some bad stuff already. Imagine if that was organised and directed. Those who are left have been crying out for leadership, for someone to tell them what to do and where to go. With that want, what they are told does not really matter – just that they are told to do something. That there's someone to blame, or some second chance to right the wrongs."

"I had not thought of that. I mean, our trip kind of defies logic and sense as well you know."

"Don't I know it. We are just going to have to take care of each other." James quickly glanced at her as he said this, but she had her back to him.

Kathryn turned her head slightly but did not meet his gaze, as she answered softly, "Like we already do, you mean?"

Then she turned fully to look at him.

James smiled at her and she smiled back and they held the look for a brief moment. After that, both took a shower and cleaned themselves up as they awaited Mr Aubrey's return.

Their anticipation was eventually satisfied with a sharp rattle on the door. James glanced at Kathryn who nodded, and he opened the door.

nineteen

the opened door revealed, as expected, a punctual Mr Aubrey, still in the same prim attire added only by a long black coat and bowler hat tucked under his arm. He directed an expectant look towards James and did not wait for an invitation to enter the room. Instead he addressed them in a clipped tone, "Are you ready?"

Kathryn pulled on her cardigan and James grabbed his thick, creased green sweater that lay on the bed, taken earlier from his pack that was stowed in the car. He put it on and answered. "Yes, thank you again. Please, Mr Aubrey, let me introduce ourselves properly, my name is James and this is my friend Kathryn."

"Pleased to meet you both. Now, shall we? We do not want to be late tonight."

James exchanged a quiet look with Kathryn and they left the room. They trod the hallway once more and took the elevator down, leaving the hotel the same way that they had entered. As they stepped out into the street, an unseasonably icy wind swept over them. Any lingering heat from the sunny day had evaporated as night had securely drawn in as they walked. It was cold and Kathryn shivered, moving closely with James, trying to share what little warmth they each could muster.

Dark shadows from the tall buildings cloaked their walk, with the streetlight coupled only modestly with the moon to produce a gloomy track through Mount Pleasant. The places that they walked by were expansive in the sense that they were tall with big windows and wide reception areas, but they had that quality in a functional rather than luxurious way. They had been built for purpose and many of them appeared to be modern offices with large tinted glass fronts and scripted signs advertising various companies that stood uniformly side by side along the street. They had little in the way of ornaments. No flowers adorned the reception and no balconies looked down upon the road.

They walked on in silence through deserted streets, crossing empty roads. No noise could be heard, and so they moved forward in silence with Mr Aubrey setting a brisk pace. After a while, they came to the end of what James surmised was the business district and entered a large concrete estate. In the midst of this estate was their destination, the church, gloriously and extravagantly lit up in the otherwise dark night air.

In keeping with the architecture of the row of offices, the church had something of a modern look about it, though it was also mixed in with classical elements of older religious buildings. It was built from orange bricks and had a white roof held up by thick pillars. Tall rectangular black windows stretched around the long walls leading to two tall identical towers on the left and right that led upwards on either side to a large brass bell, silhouetted in the sky.

Outside the church was a white cross mounted on an ebony plinth and red tassels which billowed in the wind were tied on the sides of the cross. From when the church first came into view, James could just about make out a solitarily figure in the shadows between the central two pillars. Straining his eyes, he saw a dark outline of a person standing alone in the light.

When they moved closer, the wind picked up a greater ferocity. The figure was watching them and James could see that he was smiling. Kathryn clutched at the back of his sweater as Mr Aubrey picked up the pace. They soon passed the cross and James could see the figure was a man. He was a holy man clutching in two hands a leather-bound Bible, and he addressed them in a clear deep voice as they approached.

"New converts, eh, Mr Aubrey? Welcome to Saint Mark's. You will find all that you require inside, my friends."

Mr Aubrey nodded stiffly and Kathryn smiled nervously at the man with the Bible, barely maintaining eye contact. James likewise wordlessly greeted him, as the man's eyes carefully followed them walking through the open door into the church.

The room that greeted them as they entered was lengthy and wide with many doors on either side. It was dominated by a lifelike statue of Christ on the opposite side of the entrance, his arms out stretched in welcome. The statue loomed over a large, circular marble fountain and they heard the trickling of the water. Tall bookshelves were placed sparsely between the numerous doors, and in front of them were armchairs. The carpet was dark red and the walls were painted cream. Bordered over the doors were intricately detailed paintings of various biblical scenes, including the ascension of Christ to heaven and an unsmiling Adam and Eve in the Garden of Eden.

Three women were waiting for them as they walked in. Each of them was modestly dressed in a grey skirt and a buttoned up white blouse. They were smiling, and one, the eldest of the three, who James guessed to be in her fifties or early sixties, spoke to them.

"Mr Aubrey, so nice to see you again, and you brought guests with you. Welcome to you all. We are serving the food in number two today – it is soup tonight. Go right ahead, they are all waiting for you in there."

James smiled a little uneasily, though he could not explain his discomfort. "Thank you for your hospitality. Did you say they are all waiting for us?"

The lady nodded curtly. "Yes, Mr Aubrey never misses a meeting. Eat; then we can all enjoy the sermon. The pastor has something special tonight. I think that you will be enriched here. Please, let us go and eat."

The lady swept around, flanked by her two companions and followed shortly by Mr Aubrey. James lingered with Kathryn and he whispered to her. "Are you okay?"

"I'm a little tired, to be honest. I don't know if I can take a sermon, but I guess we must if we are going to eat. I think we've probably come too far to leave now anyway. Mr Aubrey seems well thought of here and it would be unfair to embarrass him."

The quartet turned and looked at them, still smiling but quiet this time as they waited, their arms held out in front of them. After a short moment, James and Kathryn followed and were led to the final door on the left. As the six of them entered, they walked into a large room replete with numerous tables and chairs and more people than he had seen in one place since the disappearances. Spoons clinked on the edge of bowls as three or four dozen people tucked into their meal.

As soon as the door clicked shut behind them, the low murmur of conversation quietened and each individual lifted their head and watched as James and Kathryn were sat down by the ladies on the far side of the room. Mr Aubrey, on the other hand, moved off in his own way and took a seat in the centre of the room with a different group of people. They sat at a long metallic table on a fold up silver chair. The room was full of people and was lit by long blue overhead lights. A large silver vat of steaming soup was at the front of the room, presided over by a woman dressed much as the three bodies who had greeted James and Kathryn.

The silent duo among the trio of women clutched three empty bowls and moved towards the soup. One of them took a huge ladle and tipped a dollop of soup into each of the bowls. The ladies then took the food over to James and Kathryn who both thanked them quietly. They sat with their food before them and eventually the stares of other diners drifted back to their own business and the buzz of chatter rose again, albeit only to a low level.

They had taken what appeared to be the final two empty seats in the room, and six other people also sat at their table eating soup. Kathryn smiled at them but got only blank, featureless stares in response from those who caught her gaze. The other six were all men of assorted ages, who ate quietly without acknowledging the two newcomers. James looked at the other men and surmised that they knew each other as they exchanged furtive glances.

After a while, when it appeared that everyone had finished their meal, the same busy trio of women strode into the room and what little talk there was hushed in an instant. They came to a stop at the centre of the room, just in front of where the now empty vat of soup stood. All eyes looked upon them expectantly. One of the ladies, the one who had spoken earlier, moved two steps forward and surveyed what was around her, scanning the room quietly.

Then she spoke. "He is ready, please go through."

With that, the majority of the room stood up almost as one body. James felt an air of excitement enter the room. It was like an electrical current was invisibly connecting the people. He almost felt that if he reached out, he would be able to touch it. However it was an excitement he himself did not share. James felt detached from it all and he stayed seated, as did Kathryn.

The other people moved impatiently, shuffling and twitching from side to side as they made their way out of the room. Kathryn picked up the two bowls. One of the hitherto quiet women walked over to where they sat and spoke in a sweet, whispered voice. "It is okay. Leave the dishes."

Kathryn smiled at her, but it was half-hearted, James noted. *She shares the same unease.* Nonetheless, she rose first and he joined her. Slowly they joined the procession of people walking into the long reception area, crossing it and choosing another door.

The room that they entered was vast. It was big enough to hold the fifty or so people who were in there that night, but at the same time it also retained a personal, cosy quality. The room was lit by dozens of candles all sat on black, wavy stands that held five candles each. This gave the room a warm, dim glow. A large fireplace dominated the centre of one of the walls, and logs and coals flamed away sending a rich burning smell outwards. Tall curtains were drawn and outside the wind could be heard bursting and howling through the night air, rattling against the windows. A wooden stage was erected at one side of the room, upon which was two torches flickering away on either side of a lectern.

Save for the people in it, the room itself was sparsely occupied. No chairs were laid out, and no tables stood idle. There were long wooden counters that stood chest high to James. These counters were like a maze spiralling round the room, and it was against one of these that James stood beside with Kathryn slightly in front of him as they both faced the stage. The other people milled around randomly finding space where they could, waiting in small groups of no more than three or four. Long, misshapen shadows were cast upon the plush scarlet carpet and a layer of dust hung with the tension in the air, as the room waited with baited breath for what was to come. Though neither spoke of it, both James and Kathryn continued to share a feeling of uneasiness, tempered only by their comfort in one another. She moved to his side, where he stood leaning against one of the wooden counters. The fire crackled and spat sparks into the gloomy air. She brushed against his side, and he offered her a reassuring half smile, though the tired rings around his eyes betrayed his weariness.

Kathryn dropped her left hand down by her side, and slowly, softly feeling for the gap, she slipped her fingers into James' and closed them tightly. Her fingers sent a warm feeling coursing through him. He moved his free hand down and placed it over the two that were enclosed, and he gently stroked the back of her hand with his thumb.

He felt safe, almost serene. Amidst the chaos, it was a gentle moment, and he looked into Kathryn's large eyes and was grateful. He was grateful that she was here with him, grateful for her touch, grateful just for her. Whatever occurred this night, whatever uncertainty he continued to feel, this second was a moment of genuine intimacy. It was a closeness that surprised him as it stirred a long forgotten memory. However, this sense of calm proved fleeting as he could make out a figure lingering in the shadows in the darkness of the corner of the platform and still holding hands, they both watched with trepidation, waiting to listen to what was to come.

A man strode onto stage, the wooden slates creaking beneath his feet sending sprinkling clouds of dust fluttering into the gloom with each step that he took. He was dressed all in black, with smooth slacks and a crisply pressed collarless shirt. His grey hair was neatly trimmed and carefully parted at the side. Not a hair moved as he stopped at the waist high wooden lectern placed on the middle of the platform. The man pressed each of his hands upon the sides of the lectern and quietly looked out at the people before him. The room hushed so that the only remaining noise they heard was the flickering of nearby candles, the snapping of the fire, and the wind outside beating relentlessly against the windows.

James felt Kathryn's grip tighten slightly and he felt an urge rising in him to look at her, just for a second, though it was mere moments since the man had emerged before them silently demanding his attention. This was the person that they had been invited to see and whose audience James awaited with real frayed nerves. He felt an inexplicable aura of danger in the room that night, an electric menace that pervaded the air. He looked at those around him, huddled closely.

It's them.

Somehow, his fear permeated from the people that stood quietly in the hall. It was in their lonely yearning and desperate desire for answers and purpose. He sensed a volatile atmosphere and a potential for anger amongst these people.

They are ready to believe, but what will they be told?

James chided himself for making such assumptions, but try as he might, he could not shake them.

These people had come for what they had been promised – answers, an explanation and a way forward. With eager anticipation these people were ready to listen and where they felt excitement, James felt only fear.

He gently squeezed Kathryn's hand back.

The man looked out at the crowd before him, his eyes flashing in the twilight as the two great torches flamed on either side. He spoke in crystal clear tones, with a deep, booming voice that did not falter.

"Good evening. Allow me first to introduce myself to those few here who do not know me. I am Titus Domina, pastor of this church for these past two decades. We are all here to seek the answer to the vanishings that have broken our souls these last few days. Let me tell you, brothers and sisters, our souls were already broken. Some of you will not like what I have to say here tonight, and I tell you now that I can offer little comfort. I offer no freedom from pain, no solace from tribulation. But I promise the truth. More than this, I will guide you, the remnants, to the path of redemption and eternal salvation."

Domina's voice rose to a crescendo and he paused to survey the effects of his words. The crowd seemed to huddle a little closer as he spoke, and the wind rose yet more. Though the room was warm, James' arm began to burst into goose pimples. He glanced at Kathryn and saw that the hairs on her neck were standing on end as Domina continued.

"Genesis tells us of a time long since past. It tells us of a time when the old ones roamed the earth. They were fallen angels exiled to earth in punishment for their rebellion against the almighty. The old ones walked amongst our people and lay with the daughters of men, creating abominations that blighted the once green and pleasant land. These creatures were abject horrors vile in the sight of the Lord. They could not be permitted to exist. In his wisdom, the Lord beat them back with the Great Flood and cascading water crashed down destroying these beasts. The old ones, for their sins, were imprisoned in Taurus, binding them until the time just before the Great Judgement where eternal torment awaits them."

James thought of those paintings that he had seen and pictured them in his mind.

The crucifixion, the man being burnt. The mural of Eden and the large image of Christ in this very building.

Kathryn continued to squeeze his hand, though her eyes remained fixed and wide upon Domina. The pastor's words never wavered or faltered for even a syllable as he kept on speaking.

"However, the fate of these monsters shall entwine with man's once again. Prophecy foretells that they will be loosed for a short time in the latter days and all hell shall follow them. Nightmares are to be taken from our heads and put upon the dirt on the ground. God has called his people home in preparation and we who are left shall know no protection, nor shall we find a place to hide. There will be no rock, no cave where the demons will not find us. My friends, they are coming. They are making their way through the earth to the surface, scratching and clawing their way coming for us. The monsters are coming, and the whole world shall be set aflame. Where it was once drowned, now shall it be razed to the ground. None shall be spared, for the wrath of God is here and the saints themselves weep in heaven and the moon trembles at the woes that we are destined to suffer."

Monsters. There are monsters coming. He is telling us that monsters are coming for us.

He heard Kathryn gasp. Looking around the room, the quietness pressed in as all seemed to hang on Domina's words. No one moved. Their bodies were frozen in awed silence and the wind let up for a few moments. He saw the fear he felt reflected in their still bodies.

What does he want us to do? He is going to command us.

The pastor's voice was rising as he went and his words were gaining speed and volume. Kathryn's grip was strong now, and like everyone else in the room, she was unmoving.

"The tribulation is at hand and the beasts are at the gates. In the darkness they shall hunt us. In the shadows they shall stalk our steps. The monsters shall find us as we shake in fear, and it is there that they shall drag us into the pit. Until that moment we shall know neither peace nor comfort. Our thirst shall not be quenched, our desires frustrated, and though we pray for death, it shall not be granted. We will scream, my friends, and the world before us will burn. God is here no longer and we will scream. As the claws creep towards our bodies sleeping in the gloom, we shall scream, for there will be no escape from our dreams as our nightmare will reach out for us."

Kathryn edged closer still and looked at James. He could see the reflection of the candles flicker in her eyes. She shifted uneasily from one foot to the other. Almost involuntarily they began to creep backwards a step or two.

He glanced around at the other people. The groups had seemed to shift closer together as they leaned forward to where the pastor stood. They were yawning towards him as he paused before his sermon went on.

"This is how the world is ending. It has started and once the wheels have begun to move, there can be no stopping them.

We have been cut off. We are alone. From God and from each other, we have been cut off. Those damned must stand alone. They are alone against the beast. All these things shall come to pass."

Domina again paused and the crowd stood silently still holding their breath. James was now as still as any, trying to define his emotion between a mixture of shock, awe, disbelief, and revulsion. He felt a weight in the pit of his stomach and an ache in his heart. He wanted to leave and get as far away from this place as was possible. Kathryn edged closer to him and they shared a glance. The same fear he felt was etched upon her face.

She leaned closer and whispered in his ear. "James, can we go? I don't like this."

He looked at her carefully and nodded. "I don't either, but we can't just slip away. As soon as he is finished, we'll get out of here."

Kathryn looked at him wearily, her hands still entwined with his, but she returned his nod before catching her breath. "He's not even finished. He is going to tell people to do something. I don't think it's going to be good."

He held her gaze, his eyes equally wide, butterflies flapping in the pit of his stomach as the pastor finished his sermon.

"The world is doomed. It has fallen into iniquity and God has abandoned it. But my sons and daughters, I am here to tell you that there is still hope. There is still the dimmest glimmer in utter darkness and we can yet be saved. To earn the restitution of our souls we must purge the earth in fire. We must go from here this very night and set loose to burn."

Set loose to burn. These people are ready to do his will. They are frightened and they are ready to do what they are told.

"As our bodies pass from this world, we remnants must take all that is fallen with it. We have but a short time and all that is barbarous must be purged. We must go from here, taking just the clothes on our backs, and we must burn. Do not let mercy steady your hand. This world has been judged and it will be taken apart, for that is His will. There is yet time for us, but we must fill the distance between now and our judgment with God's work. We must purge the idolaters. Only then can we escape the lake of fire that shall be the fate of the worldly people. There is no other way. We have been lustful and full of pride and God has frowned upon us. That is why we have been left behind whilst our righteous brothers and sisters have been raptured. But we have one final chance left, one final task to save our immortal souls."

James held his breath, his heart thumping.

"For that, you must join me."

At the end of his proclamation, Domina stretched out his arms in front, imploring those before him, his hands shaking. He had spoken for hardly anytime at all, but the impact was significant on those in the church that night. Many of the listeners moved closer together, some slower than others, hinting at hesitation, but most moved forward eagerly forming a mass in the presence of the pastor, creating a band of people seething together as one.

As those others went forward, James tugged Kathryn's hand, sweeping her quickly but quietly to the door behind the mass of people. As Domina individually addressed the crowd before him, James carefully pushed open the door as quietly as possible and they slipped out into the reception area ready to take their leave. However, standing in the centre of the long hallway was Mr Aubrey and the lady who had greeted them on their entrance. They both stood unmoved, arms placed out before them and their eyes fixed on James and Kathryn.

Kathryn addressed them in a nervous tone. "Hey, Mr Aubrey, interesting evening."

He looked back unblinkingly and spoke in the same clipped voice. "Going somewhere, miss?"

James looked at him. "Just back to the hotel. I guess we will see you there later?"

"There is work to do this night, James, great work. We all have a role to play."

"Well, we have an early start tomorrow, many miles to cover, you know. I think we will be getting off."

"The hotel will not be there much longer. Didn't you listen? We have been set to burn and that is what we must do. There shall be no more adulterers crossing my door."

Kathryn moved closer to James and looked at Mr Aubrey. "What did you do?" She asked quietly.

"What needs to be done."

At this point, the woman beside Mr Aubrey spoke, her voice harsh and low. "You cannot leave."

James hesitated. "Excuse me?"

The woman fixed him with a glare and the corners of her lips turned upward into a thin smile. "You cannot leave. We cannot suffer an unregenerate to live." Behind them in the room where Domina had spoke, a loud and guttural roar filled the place that they departed, as the lady continued. "They are waiting for you."

The door opened and Domina stepped out, flanked by several people on either side. James moved to stand in front of Kathryn blocking the pastor. The wind whistled and the fire crackled for a moment, and then there was silence in the hallway. Even the water in the fountain stilled. There was utter silence. A smile crept slowly over Domina's face, but still no one moved, seemingly waiting on a prompt. James tried to suppress a rising panic.

They are ready. They are ready to move at the slightest inclination.

Kathryn's breathing got a little heavier, louder and quicker. James looked around all around him, his eyes flickering from one place to another unable to settle on any one image or person. His heart thumped and his face flushed an angry red.

Then he spoke simple words. "No. This is not happening."

Again he clasped Kathryn's hand, forcefully this time, and glaring at those in front of him, James led the two of them purposefully forward, slamming his shoulder against Mr Aubrey sending him spinning a few involuntary steps backwards. Then Domina spoke and James stopped with his back to him as he listened.

"Let them go. They will not get far and there is nowhere for them to go. Only misery and torment awaits them. We are not the only ones who creep in the night. They are damned, and they will be found by those who dwell in the night, and you can be as sure as the fact that I am standing here, their fate is sealed. They will be taken, eventually. Let them go, for now."

He then directed his words towards James and Kathryn, raising his voice. "Beware those noises in the dark. They are out there and they know your name, James. They will reach for you both."

This time it was Kathryn that did the urging. She pulled James forward towards the door. They had crossed the concrete car park before they let go of each other's hands. Hurrying as they went, their shoes slapping the concrete noisily, they moved out of sight of the church. It was only then that they began to talk to each other again, James first.

"We need to work out what we are going to do. We obviously can't stay at the hotel, but dare we go back for the car?"

Kathryn nodded. "We at least have a start on them and we could get back there before they do. I think it's worth the risk, because we need to get the hell out of here as quick as is humanly possible. What do you think?"

"I am tired, Kathryn. I'm really tired. We should stick to the plan and find somewhere to bed down. Somewhere out of the way like your uncle's house. Somewhere no one will be able to get to us. There must be somewhere like that close by but still out of town."

"I agree. We should take the back roads and hope to get lucky somewhere and come across a place in the woods or something. Then we can get going tomorrow, but we definitely need to put some miles between here and ourselves. Let's get to the car, quickly."

"Come on, Kathryn."

They moved rapidly through the streets, keeping largely to the shadows. They did not speak of what transpired in the church.

It was too much, too much to take in.

Kathryn did not attempt to talk of it either, and it was as if both were silently considering what Domina had said. It was clear, James knew, that neither of them liked what he had laid out, but at the same time it was an answer. It was a confident explanation of the disappearances, and no one else had offered a clearer theory, not to say one offered with as much force. He hurried his steps a little, and they were soon back outside the hotel and at the car.

Throwing open the door, they both clambered aboard and he revved the engine spinning the wheels as they tore off. Somewhere in the distance he could hear a low rumble. They had left the church and were loose in the streets.

They had begun.

The thought panicked James, and for a while he drove blindly around the roads of Mount Pleasant unsure of where to go. A smouldering scent of burning reached his senses. He turned corner after corner seeking a route, any route, out of town. The noise of people grew ever louder and was matched by a series of loud crashes and deep bangs and thumps.

Eventually they came to the outskirts of town and they chanced upon a dirt track leading between a cluster of trees, disappearing into thick darkness. As James turned into it he exchanged a hopeful look with Kathryn. He nudged the lights onto full beams as they drove down the uneven road, rattling along. The track was barely wide enough for the car and the trees were thick on either side. He could barely see much further than the immediate area in front of the vehicle, but the track was mainly straight, bending only occasionally and very slightly. The farther they went, the more the disquiet in his gut lessened, although it did not disappear completely.

After a few uncomfortable miles they came to a gate, beyond which the track narrowed to a point where the car would not be able to pass. He stopped and looked at her. "Do we go back?"

"Back to town? Are you joking? Besides, it's too far and it is definitely too late. I say we risk it. That track has to go somewhere. You don't just put a gate in the middle of nowhere, you know."

James nodded. Going back was not very appealing to him either. "I guess we're walking then."

"I guess we are."

twenty

James unhooked the chipped and rusty metal latch on the wooden gate and pushed it judderingly forward, holding it open for Kathryn. The track was dusty and it was lit by only a couple of crooked orange orbs hanging from bent streetlights long since neglected but remarkably still purring with what appeared to be the final gasps of its energy. On either side of the track were neglected fields of straggled grass populated by the odd tree, misshapen and wild with arching branches of green leaves that draped along the ground. An almost tangible smell of blackberries filled the air and James felt as if he could almost taste the fruit amidst the untidy brambles beside the grass.

A full moon hung imperiously above, silently watching them walk together in quiet contemplation. The day had been long; they had travelled many miles and they had much on their mind. The crickets began to chirp and the wind was cold. James had longed for answers when he was back in Cedar Falls, now those offered seemed of little comfort. Beyond the fate of all things, he again thought about his purpose.

Do I hope to find Danielle, or do I hope that she is gone? Do I hope that the pastor is right? Of course I hope the pastor is wrong. He reminded himself. But the thought nagged.

Those things he spoke of, those creatures in the night, what did he mean?

James shuddered unable to tell whether it was the cold or his own misgivings at what Domina said that caused it.

I do not believe him, I do not.

But he wanted to get inside. He wanted badly to find safe shelter where he could close his eyes.

If the pastor was right then those that had been taken were the lucky ones. Have I been mistaken to mourn them? Maybe the departed are somewhere above, grieving my destiny. Perhaps they don't know or care.

James could not answer his own questions. Something about Domina's words resonated within him, but they were just so unbelievable, so fanciful. He did not like the way that they made him feel. He did not like the morbid seduction of his claims or the way in which he pried upon people's fear. He did not follow his line of thought. Whatever, he wanted to get inside and quickly, because his weariness again ached his bones and tired his spirit.

He glanced at Kathryn who was also quiet with a thoughtful expression. He left it a moment, before talking.

"The end of the world. This is it. So, do you buy it Kathryn? I'll tell you what though, since this thing began, all I have seen is confusion and sadness – and that's when I've seen people at all. Those who emerged from that hall had neither. They really believe that they know what has happened and worse, they are certain they know what to do about it. I think Domina got them excited about the forthcoming destruction; he seemed to almost revel in it what he thinks is coming."

Kathryn nodded. "Yeah, they did. I have read a little about the apocalypse and the wrath of God and the seven seals and all that. Some Christians believe the destruction of the world is just a precursor to the reign of Christ and the saints. Many of them believe that before this blessed reign, the world will become so mired in wickedness that God will have no choice but to judge it."

James frowned. "Judge the world? Not the people but the world?"

"Both. And so he does. Lord, how he does. He sends down a series of judgments. The seas turn to blood and moon darkens … I forget all of them but there are around twenty in all. Eventually, it ends in Armageddon, man's final battle, where we pretty much kill each other until there's hardly anyone left. But before all of this occurs, God calls those who truly believe in him home in an event called the Rapture. This is to protect them, because after they are gone, hell tips into the earth. The remnants that are left are considered to deserve everything that they – that we – are going to get. Then, after all of this is done and the world is destroyed, paradise is to follow."

"I guess I can see why people would look for that change, especially if they were miserable. It sounds brutal to me. Do you believe in that stuff?"

Kathryn sighed wistfully and brushed her hair from her cheek, placing it carefully behind her ear. "Ah, James, I'm a worldly girl. I love the Springsteen concerts and the *Star Wars* films. I love my red dress and my strappy shoes. I love my Winnie the Pooh bed covers and my poster of a cute dog. A warm bath on a cold night, a cup of cocoa. It's the look of the leaves when they turn orange and the first glint of snow in winter. There's a lot to love, I think."

James smiled and slowed his footsteps. "That's lovely, Kathryn."

"Funnily enough I never was sure of these things before. But I look back now and wonder how are we not supposed to be utterly in love with all of them? So much of what we see and have is unspeakably dear, so hopelessly and desperately lovely, and I can't accept that they are to be destroyed, especially not by he who created it."

"I don't think Domina shared the same joy."

"How are we supposed to hate this place? I won't believe it, I won't. Those people spoke so callously of the destruction of the entire works of man, everything we have achieved, how far we have come, all of our glorious, pointless, self-created problems and delusions of grandeur. They see the eradication of this as something divine, something great. The destruction of everything we made is supposed to be something that we deserve?"

They walked on. Kathryn nibbled at her bottom lip that shook slightly before she continued.

"Well that is not holy and that is not just. If there is a God, how can he just take us from our homes? How, when we were happy and had come so far? But of course, I don't really believe it's the end. I cannot believe that a man like Domina can know the mind of God. The God I believed in was loving, patient, and merciful. He didn't just take people away. I think there is some other explanation, though I cannot offer it to you."

"But it nags at you, doesn't it? The thought that it may be true, I mean."

"It does. But I have faith in us and the world."

They pressed on a while in silence, the grass bristling quietly in the breeze. Her pale eyes were bloodshot and contained in them a mix of sadness and weariness. The sandals on her feet flapped against her soles, making a rhythmic clapping sound as they strolled and James thought about what she had said. He wanted to protect her faith in the world from such dark times. He had a distant memory of when he had felt something similar. A vague feeling crept over him, slowly at first then a little faster. It was a memory when he too had a love of the world. It was an affection for the hometown that he had left so long ago and for the life that had passed him by. He thought about what she had said and the memory twisted into a feeling of regret.

"The truth is, recently I haven't felt the way you have. I seemed to have spent most of my life trying to escape the world.

I read a lot, watch TV and films, that kind of thing. Through these stories I can live another life, far from wherever I am. Those other worlds people made were so vivid and close that it seemed like all I had to do was reach out and touch them. Sometimes I desperately hoped that the places I dreamed of were real and that maybe I would fall into some strange land and walk along the pier of a faraway world."

He walked with his head down, not looking at Kathryn. His words were spoken quietly.

"Those stories made me feel. They made me believe and even belong somehow. I felt more at home in those created places than I did in the world around me and there were times when I would have willingly traded this world for that. Now it seems as if this world has gone, and even if we can recover, even if there is some way that we can claw back everything that we have lost and somehow begin to build again, it won't be the same. Things will never be the same again and we won't fully know what it is that we have lost until the end."

"It's okay, James. I think a lot of the time people don't appreciate what they have until it's gone."

"It's silly and I'm not making much sense. But without this world, there is nothing to escape from. Those snatched moments of pleasure somewhere else, those dreams, they are not possible without the old world, without our world."

Kathryn brushed against him gently. "You see things differently now?"

"I think so. The truth of the matter is, and as silly as it sounds after all that we've seen, I'm enjoying walking here with you tonight. I'm enjoying your company. Perhaps not enough for the world as we know it to fall apart, but it is pleasant, you know?"

Kathryn smiled and little creased dimples appeared either side of her mouth and she patted his arm with gentle affection. They trudged on in silence until by lucky chance, the fields spread around a small house beside a large barn. At once their spirits lifted and their steps seemed less heavy. The house was a single storey building with chipped white paintwork and slatted windows and a long, spacious porch. It had a homely rustic look with a chained bench hanging over a platform outside the front door. Ivy crept all around the house and baskets of overflowing flowers hung in the corners of the porch area. Behind was a tall barn coloured brown with a slanted roof built from long planks of wood.

They passed through a white picket fence which was surrounded by a neatly trimmed lawn that led towards the house.

Her spirits rising, Kathryn proclaimed happy words. "Oh, this looks perfect James. I guess we got lucky." She laughed to herself. "I guess we got really lucky."

The path to the house comprised of a series of grey slabs leading to a small number of wooden white steps that ascended to the porch where a bench rocked to and fro in the wind. The white paint was faded and chipped in all manner of places and the wood on the handrail of the creaking stairs was rough and un-planed. He opened a screen and tapped lightly on the door and waited for a while. There was no response, so he tapped a little louder. Again there was no reply. The temperature dipped once more, and now it was beneath chilly and had entered cold. Wind rushed through the grass around the house and the rusted metal of the chained bench heaved. It was dark and the street lights were far behind them. Only the moon and the stars lit their position as they waited no more. James tentatively nudged the door. With a creak it swung open and they went through.

Inside the house it was dark and black shapes were all that he could make out. Kathryn stretched her arm across the wall, running her fingers over bobbled wallpaper. Her reaching ended when she came across that which was sought and a switch was flicked illuminating the house in an orange glow.

They found themselves in a modest abode, though it was cosy, giving the little house a homely feel. They were in a living room with a large white sofa pointed towards a television set. There was a small table beside it with purple flowers standing upright in a vase. A little book cabinet stood beside the door that they had entered through, containing novels with heavily creased spines. Looking out over the living room was a kitchen area with sand-coloured surfaces and units. Along the windowsill lay a number of cookery books, crooked and unevenly placed. A table was pushed up against the counters, and place mats were set for two potential diners.

The house was comfortably warmer than the air outside and he noted that it bore the hallmarks of place well maintained by its owner. *They cared for it. They kept it nice and neat.* This was someone's home and he felt for a moment that he was intruding upon an intimate place. *It's somewhere personal, a home that mattered to someone. They took pride in it and made it their own.*

There were two doors on the opposite side of the entrance and Kathryn poked her head around each of them before returning. "One bathroom, one bedroom. This is a nice place."

James nodded. "I like it too."

"I am tired, James. I think I'm going to get ready for bed."

"I'm going to stay up for a little while, I think."

"Okay," Kathryn replied and she squeezed his shoulder.

He watched her disappear into the bathroom before slipping off his shoes and socks allowing air to breeze pleasantly around his toes as he spread them out. He stretched and his shoulders crackled. Though he was tired, James was not yet ready to sleep. Images of Domina and Danielle swam round his head and ideas formed and drifted away before coming back again unfulfilled and incoherent.

He stepped into the kitchen and opened one of the cupboards at random. Inside he found a black oil lamp. It was cube shaped with a thick metal handle that swept around the top. Next to it was stored a box of matches and James picked up both. He struck a match and then pushed open the front door and stepped back outside, carefully lighting the lamp as he went.

Breathing in deeply, James tasted the fresh night air. It was still cold but not uncomfortable, and the sweet smell of the grass soothed him as he moved along the porch towards the swinging bench. He placed the burning lamp on a hook on top of the bench and it emitted as much modest warmth as it did light, and he sat down and rocked back and forth slowly.

The cushioned seat was even more comfortable than he had hoped for, and the chain creaked as the bench gently swayed to and fro. He pulled his feet up and they dangled just a few inches from the wooden panelled deck as he sat there thinking.

We are close to Pickering. Likely we will make it tomorrow. Journey's end. It's so close. Tomorrow I might see Danielle.

The simple truth of this weighed heavily upon him, and the doubts came creeping back. He rocked back and forth a little quicker. He was suddenly afraid – afraid for his future, afraid for his prospects, afraid that he was leading Kathryn on pointless, far-fetched quest that would achieve nothing.

Maybe I'm just tired. I don't know anymore.

He had sat for a few minutes when the screen door opened at the end of the porch and Kathryn stepped out. She gripped a mug of steaming chocolate in each hand. After offering one to a grateful James, she sat down next to him, yawning and sending the bench swaying a little. She pulled her knees up to her chest, hugging them, and together, she and James looked out over the lawn and the white picket fence beyond. Even in the gloom, it was clear that someone had loved this garden once. The grass was evenly cut and a procession of flowers, identical to the ones in the vase inside by the sofa, stood proudly silhouetted in the dark.

The night had fully drawn as they sat and his panic mellowed as he sipped the piping hot drink. He found himself thankful for the respite of the cottage, however temporary it might be. They were away from the hysteria of the church and the dangerous cries of the city. He leaned back and wondered to himself, if the owner of this house was still here, would they even notice the state of the world?

Would they know that people had disappeared? Would they know of the chaos that threatened to unfold in the town that was so close to their home?

But sitting there, none of that mattered. It was as if there was nothing beyond the picket fence. In the whole world there was just him and Kathryn, and at that moment there were no troubles, no questions, and no sorrows. The fear that washed over him seconds earlier had flowed elsewhere.

The oil lamp just above the swinging seat continued to send out a tiny glow of warm orange. The crickets continued their nightly chorus, emitting a distant stream of background noise as Kathryn rested her head on his shoulder. They sat in a comfortable but weary silence until the night turned utterly dark, blanketing the sky in a jet black cover.

They had come a long way since the mansion and Mount Pleasant, and they were both tired. James felt the fatigue of one who had travelled for so long and come so far. The idle days of sitting and reading on a warm afternoon, the lazy tedious hours of waiting for half past five were long gone, though they had only been a few days ago. The comfort of a known and predictable life was lost in the midst of constant motion.

But these fleeting moments of rest and respite, however brief, were becoming time he treasured. A feeling of contentment had slipped into James taking him by surprise as he sat on the veranda with Kathryn. It was a rare glimpse of normal life. The chaos of the outside world seemed a distant nightmare and they could be anyone, at any time in man's history, as they sat there. It was an instant of familiarity in a strange time. He sat back and savoured it.

Then, Kathryn squeezed his arm and spoke in a hushed, wondrous tone. "James, it's so dark. There is no moon. It is a clear night and there is no moon. There are no stars either."

The sky was perfectly black, unbroken and constant. There was no pin-pricking of stars or illumination of any kind. The sole light in the vicinity of the house was the single oil lamp on the veranda. The night air was completely empty, and staring into it was like looking into the abyss.

The contentment was fleeting departing quickly, and James sat open mouthed feeling a chill, though the air was perfectly still. "It's eerie, like there's nothing there. It's as if the whole universe has been sucked away."

They moved closer together and looked upwards as slowly the picture changed. From some distant point within the still sea of black, a tiny dot of shimmering red slowly emerged. Gradually, the dot grew and grew. All the while a crimson aura flowed around the spherical body. It began to expand more quickly, appearing to get ever closer to earth and where they sat. The orb was joined by another and then another and another. Before long the entire sky was filled with the approaching bodies, small at first and then growing.

"James," Kathryn said, panic rising in her voice.

As the orbs approached the ground, penetrating the atmosphere, an increasing rushing sound began to drown out the crickets. The closer they got, the clearer they became. They were flaming ferociously with vivid shades of red pulsating from its core. The orb seemed to hang, tantalisingly, just above the land like a low cloud, just for the merest second, before gracefully but rapidly dropping to the ground below.

The orbs rained down somewhere in the distance beyond the house, whooshing all around them. Rather than elicit panic, or fear, or terror, both felt a measure of wonderment as they beheld the torrent of fire raining onto the earth. James was struck by the spectacle of it as the orbs raced towards the ground with streaming crimson flames rushing downwards.

His disbelief suspended the horror of the display and Kathryn remained transfixed and still beside him.

They sat for a while watching, quietly, breathlessly, in awe of what fell before them. The fire was dropping all around them, illuminating trials that they blazed in the dark. Wisps of smoke rose skyward from somewhere in the distance. No matter how regularly the fireballs fell, still more continued to bombard the land. Although none dropped close to where they sat, the orbs just kept coming, falling seemingly without pattern. He watched them fall; they were doubtlessly destructive, but there was a majestic beauty about them. There was a grace and as he stared, he felt a quiet acceptance grow within him.

If this is the end, it doesn't matter anymore. Nothing I can do will make a difference. Nothing can be done against the inevitable.

After a long time watching the scene, they both tore themselves away and moved back inside the house. James lingered by the sofa, but Kathryn ushered him into the bedroom, where they both stepped inside, slightly dazed, each inarticulate with shock and awe. Kathryn moved towards the window and pulled shut the flat blinds that hung there. Intermittent flashes of red flitted into the room as they got ready to sleep.

"James, what the hell is going on?"

He rubbed his eyes. "I don't know."

There were no words left to speak, and for a moment they shared an awed silence before she departed to the bathroom. In the meantime he found a spare blanket and sheets in an ornately carved wooden trunk that sat at the end of the bed. He carefully laid out the sheets out on the floor in the small space beside the bed as Kathryn re-emerged with a baggy grey T-shirt that fell just above her bare knees.

She looked at him wearily. "James, it's a large bed. Come on."

Another ball of fire fell somewhere close outside, slipping another flash of red into the room as James replied. "I'm sorry. Thanks, Kathryn."

He removed his T-shirt and trousers, leaving just his loose fitting red boxer shorts as Kathryn turned out the light. They slipped into bed together, and outside the rain of fire continued to cascade downward, sweeping into the distance. As she pulled the covers close, they lay considering what they had seen.

Kathryn lay on her side, facing him. "Is this how it ends, James?"

"I don't know. But what I do know is that the world is not ours anymore, if it ever was. I'm just grateful we have made it this far."

Kathryn frowned. "You think this is it then."

Then, as unexpected as it had started, so too was the sudden nature of its ending. Without notice the shooting sounds of the orbs silenced and the red light of the fire stopped flashing into the room. A measure of calm returned to the night sky and to the two of them, and soon after the light of the moon began to again creep into the room where they lay awake in the darkness. The house had survived the onslaught, at least for now, as utter silence invaded in its place.

The heat of the bedroom contrasted with the chill of the night as they tucked up together underneath a double duvet. The pale light of the moon glinted through the gaps in the blinds illuminating beams of dust, which hung motionlessly in the air. The crickets had been silenced, and neither of them could hear a single sound outside. Kathryn turned on her side, her head resting delicately on a plump white pillow, her brown hair tied back and the covers pulled up just above the curve of her breasts.

Looking at him, she whispered quietly, "What really happened with Danielle?"

He turned his head and looked back at Kathryn, and for the first time he was struck by how pretty she was. Her skin was smooth around tiny brown freckles. Her eyes were weary, but they conveyed a gentle kindness, and her tone was soft and caring. He turned away looking up at the ceiling, though he barely saw it. He closed his eyes for a second and conjured Danielle in his mind, tracing the outline of her body in the gloom. When he reopened his eyes, they misted over for a second.

Kathryn broke the silence, again speaking in a hushed and hesitant voice. "You don't have to tell me if you don't want to."

Beneath the covers, she reached for his hand, slowly and tentatively. He took it and their fingers linked. Her palm pressed warmly against his and her hold was soft. He smiled at her and began to talk in the dim light of the witching hour.

"I read a story once that was written over a hundred years ago. It was about two lovers who lived in a small town in Germany, and everywhere they looked, they saw misery and pain. They were distant from the other townsfolk and but for each other, they couldn't relate to anyone."

She squeezed his hand just a little more. "That's sad, James. What happened to them?"

"Once they realised what they had, the two lovers believed that they needed to protect it from an unfriendly world. So, forsaking everything to do with the town, they gave up all of their possessions and began a simple life in a hut that they built upon a large branch of a great oak tree in the thick of the woods."

"So they had nothing but each other?"

"Nothing at all. They lived in the hut with only the richness of each other's company. There they were, happy in their exile. But after a time, simply living apart was no longer enough, and they still didn't feel safe. While they had any link to the town, they believed that the sanctity of their love was in danger. Eventually, they burned the ladder that joined the hut to the rest of the world, cutting themselves off completely. They were happy again, their love seemingly protected and safe. However in burning the ladder, they severed their connection to food and slowly, they began to starve. In a kind of exquisite pain, they curled up in a final embrace and slipped away in each other's arms."

"That's terrible, James."

"I loved Danielle – I did – but I didn't burn the ladder, and out of some foolish and selfish desperation, I clambered down and ran back to the town. I left her. For a really long time, I wondered every day if I should have stayed in the tree house, because what I had up there felt far better than what I found below. She should have been enough for me to stay. But I chose my own way and my own ambition and I left Pickering to move away. And where did it take me? To a shop in Cedar Falls. I should have stayed with her."

Kathryn looked at him with sadness in her eyes and said quietly. "And now what? And now you're ready to starve? There's no salvation in that. It's a desperate waste of a life, of two lives even. You don't have to choose either the town or the hut. You don't have to make the choice. Don't you see?"

He exhaled and the glaze in his eyes softened. The ceiling he looked at slowly blurred into view as he spoke with equally quiet words. "What about you, Kathryn? It's not that I'm not happy you are here with me. I am, believe me, I really am. The time we've spent together may have been short, but I'm truly happy that you're here with me. But still, why are you coming? I have no plan. I can offer no guarantee of destination. I don't know what I'm doing or how it will end. I certainly don't know what to do next after getting to Pickering."

Kathryn lay on her back and sighed heavily, pausing for a second. "My life has not turned out as I hoped it would. I've always tried to be positive and take joy where I can find it, but I have never really held onto happiness for very long. It was always so fleeting. But I was able to realise that I had it when I did. Those times when I was happy, I knew it and I could savour it, even if I knew that it would be soon gone. That's the secret I think. You shouldn't try to clasp happiness and clutch it as tightly as you can for fear that it may get away. Just watch it fly. Let it fly and enjoy its beauty even if it does pass. It's still happiness whatever it looks like and wherever it goes."

James shifted slightly in the bed. "It's just that, you get this vision in your mind, this picture of a life stretching out in front of you, and it's beautiful and mysterious and exciting. It's everything that you've ever wanted. And then you don't get to live that life, you live another one instead and it's none of those things the dream promised. It hurts so much to lose it."

Kathryn turned again to face him, speaking softly in the dark.

"We have come so far and seen so much. I don't know if we are the lucky ones or the cursed few who have been left behind. But I know that right now I feel that I have been uncommonly blessed. I am not one to question that blessing, I'm just happy to enjoy it and be grateful for what it brings, whoever has sent it and whatever it means. I don't know if we will get to where we are going. I don't know if there will be a happy ending. Maybe it doesn't matter. But I hope that we get there. I hope Danielle is okay. I hope that you will be as well."

James smiled sadly at her and let go of her hand. She adjusted her body as he slipped his arm around her and pulled her close. "I hope you'll be okay as too. It does not seem likely though does it, a happy ending?"

Kathryn lay on her front and gently put her head upon his bare chest. Their bodies pressed together and her ankle crossed over his, entwining them, and for the merest second, her bare thigh brushed against his. James stroked Kathryn's shoulder and she snuggled up closer to him.

Though they both shut their eyes in the quiet darkness, neither went to sleep for a long time after.

twenty-one

they woke the next morning entwined in the same intimate position, James first. He remained still as Kathryn purred softly in her sleep. Her nose twitched slightly, and her toes wriggled against the back of his knee. Sunlight filtered into the bedroom, making it pleasantly warm and giving the morning a hazy feel. Her hair tickled against his chest and he could feel her body gradually rise and fall against his as she breathed. Outside he could hear the creak of the bench swinging freely in the wind and the birds were twittering sweetly as if it was just another day.

James breathed in deeply and smiled to himself.

It's like a normal, warm and happy late summer's morning. If I had a cup of tea and a newspaper I could stay here with her for many hours like any normal couple. But we are not a couple, and I know I'm deluding myself.

The truth of this lessened his happiness and it seemed that the sunlight dimmed just a little.

A normal summer morning is going to be a stranger for a long time. This unlikelihood was increased by the possibility that today, before he again feel asleep, he might see Danielle.

After so long living in my memories, I may finally see her in the flesh.

James felt his insides turn. But right now, he found it surprisingly easy to put such concerns to one side. He was happy, and though it might soon pass, he strove to savour its taste.

Fluttering her eyes open, Kathryn woke with a sigh and a smile. She lifted her head from his chest and, stretching out, she looked at him rubbing her eyes. "Good morning!" she said cheerfully.

James smiled back. "Hi."

Kathryn pulled a face as she rolled out bed, her grey T-shirt flapping and her brown hair buffed up and straggly. She yawned and peeked through the blinds and out the window. Pushing up her hair, Kathryn smiled to herself.

They shared a comfortable silence in the quiet warmth of the bright morning. Gathering themselves for the day ahead, they briefly went their separate ways as they dressed and cleaned themselves up. They used their time in a leisurely manner and, unrushed, reunited at the table in the living area, they ate a hearty breakfast of slightly stale toast and jam, with a glass of orange juice from a carton. From this meal they discussed their situation, Kathryn speaking first.

"So, we are, what, one hundred, one hundred and fifty miles or so away from Pickering?"

"Yeah, that sounds about right. We should make it there today. I'm not sure of the time now, but we should get there before dark. The roads off the freeway are a little winding and cannot be crossed quickly, especially if they are blocked, which I guess is very possible."

"Not to worry. We'll make it by early afternoon!"

"Then all that there will be left to do is find Danielle. I've not seen her in years and she could literally be anywhere in Pickering. It's a small town, though. Thank God for small mercies." James hesitated before continuing. "Kathryn, what are you going to do if I find her?"

"I was going to ask you the same question, but we can cross that bridge when we come to it."

He paused again and lowered his tone, looking at the table. "You won't just leave, will you? You'll stay around for a bit?"

Kathryn smiled. It was a different smile than the one she'd woken up with, and though he could not read the essence of the difference, he noticed that it was there and it troubled him. She left the question hanging and James dropped it, though the idea did not travel too far from his thoughts. Instead, he picked up the dishes and washed them up in the sink. Kathryn stood next to him and dried up the plates and glasses with a thick brown cloth. She hummed a tune as she did it. Unable to really help himself, he quietly began to form the words to the song she hummed. As he sang, Kathryn began to move from foot to foot, dancing slowly.

"She packed my bags last night, pre-flight. Zero hour, 9 a.m. And I'm gonna be high as a kite by then. And I think it's gonna be a long, long time. Der, der, der, der, I'm a rocket man."

Kathryn giggled as she moved. "You really can't sing, James, bless you."

They finished their duties quickly in jovial spirits and prepared to leave the house. James took his time and lingered longer than he would normally have. He felt a strange affinity for the place in the short time that he had spent there, much more so than the mansion that had belonged to Kathryn's uncle.

This house is a glimpse of a normal life. It was a home, well worn but tenderly cared for. In the few hours that we have spent here, it is as if the disappearances have never happened.

He had woken up happy and optimistic. The morning was bright and the weather warm and the day seemed to offer all kinds of tantalising possibilities.

Eventually, they were both ready to leave. They were well fed and clean and had a clear destination in mind, though no clue exactly what they would find there. His hometown was close at hand and he had not been back in a long time.

I wonder if the Trent Street Cinema is still standing and if the beech trees continue to wave in Oakbridge. Will I still feel that weight in my stomach when we approach the turnoff? I wonder if Picking is the same as I remember it.

James shook such thoughts from his mind. Pickering was still a distance away, and he and Kathryn had first to reach the car beyond the pathway that they had walked down the night before. There were still many miles to travel and he had no idea where Danielle might be.

What if she has gone? What if I have travelled so far, bringing Kathryn along with me, for nothing? What if she does not want to see me?

He found no answers, but he sought his resolve and the questions were replaced with a determination that he was scarcely aware that he was capable of and he knew as he walked that his options ran only one way.

I have to see this plan out. I must see it through and take it to the end. For better or worse, Pickering is our destination, and there I – we – must go. Whether I want to or not, whether it makes me happy and is the right choice is no longer important. I have made my plan and it must be followed through until the end.

Redoubled with this conviction, James opened the front door and he and Kathryn crossed the steps and moved beyond the white picket fence. James took one last look at the house.

Will I ever again feel as normal as I did in the time that we have spent here? Will I again feel the comfort that I felt last night?

He shook away such concerns and walked with a determined stride as they came back the way that they had travelled the previous night.

They walked in silence and James felt a brief sense of awkwardness. They had shared something intimate last night, and the prospect of idly chatting the morning away seemed more forced. He stayed quiet. He had shared his innermost feelings with her, something that he had not done with anyone in a long time. Suddenly he found nothing to resume conversation with her and they walked along in silence. He fretted to himself.

Have I told her too much? It felt natural last night. It was not forced or contrived, and she had shared things with me. No, I'm glad that I told her what I did, and I'm thankful that Kathryn confided in me in return.

James chided himself for being silly. They had shared a happy song and a smile over breakfast, and though he could think of nothing to say now, it did not matter. He glanced at her and the unease melted away as Kathryn walked with a spring in her step as she looked with a quiet wonderment at the passing fields. He followed her gaze and saw the effects of the previous night's celestial activities. Huge swathes of grass were flattened and darkly charred, the edges of the turf singed and discoloured. A scent of burnt turf filled the air.

"My God, James. This is just unbelievable."

"I know what you mean. Now we've slept on it, I still can't get my head around what we saw. It was like something from the Old Testament."

"Yeah, it kind of adds credence to what Domina said, doesn't it? I wonder if it will happen again tonight. I mean, Christ, anything could happen these days. Exciting, isn't it?"

Kathryn winked at James and added a little skip to her step. He laughed, as they again trampled the well trodden straw path which led to the car. By the time they had arrived at the vehicle, the sun had nearly reached its apex. Using the slightly wider space in front of the gate, James turned the car around, flattening some of the glass as he manoeuvred in three points, mauling with the heavy steering wheel. Then, facing the way that they had first travelled, they started again along the dirt track and made their way back onto the freeway, where

James directed the car east and towards the general direction of Pickering.

As they rose in speed on the flat empty and straight road, Kathryn let out a roar of delight and though he was nervous, James could not help but feed off her enthusiasm. They were on their way again.

The final leg of the journey had begun.

They had not driven far when James pulled into a gas station. They were on an ascending road that climbed above Mount Pleasant, and the station jutted out on a large flat platform halfway up the hill they were climbing. As James came to a halt beside one of the four pumps, he noticed that the custodian of the station was still there. Perched upon a rocking chair was a middle-aged man with rough stubble on his face, a straw hat, and a red and white chequered shirt above tight fitting jeans. A double-barrel shotgun lay upon his lap. Though he did not rise from his seat, the man studied them watchfully as they parked.

James got out of the car and slowly approached the man, who stroked his gun methodically. James greeted him. "Hi. Mind if I fill up the car?"

He eyed him warily for a long while before replying. "No problem. Going to have to get the money up front, though. Had a few drive off on me, if you can believe such a thing."

"Okay, that's fine. Is fifty dollars all right?" James fumbled about his pocket and pulled out his wallet. Unclipping it open, he pulled out a fifty and held it out for the man. The man hesitated, still gripping the weapon, and then took it and nodded.

"That will do nicely. Sorry to appear rude, it's a funny time, ain't it? Had some crazy folks come my way just lately. Let me fill her up for you."

"Thank you."

The man moved over towards the car and tipped his hat at Kathryn as she got out of the car smiling at him. Leaning the shotgun up against the pumps, he unhooked the nozzle and went about his service. James moved to the side of the station and leaned against a crash barrier as he looked down on Mount Pleasant below. Kathryn came to his side and they both gazed at the town at the bottom of the hill. Ugly black clouds of smoke billowed into the sunny air puffing out from numerous places.

Mount Pleasant is burning.

Most of the tall buildings were flaming as the fire danced high into the skyline. At their distance from the scene, the inferno burned in silence. It was beautiful even and he could feel its warmth lap against his cheeks.

Kathryn slipped her hand into his and together they stood there quietly watching the spectacle. Presently, the man completed his work and left James and Kathryn alone for a moment as he waited patiently a couple of steps behind them. After a while, the man placed his hand on James' shoulder, snapping him back to attention. Still holding his gun, he smiled at James. Thanking him, James let go of Kathryn's hand and they both got in the car. The man retook his seat and began to rock slowly as they drove back onto the road and further up the hill, away from Mount Pleasant and its fires.

After a few miles, the incline levelled off and the road straightened out. They now rocketed along, manoeuvring beyond loose debris of broken cars and an upturned truck. Again an occasional car passed by on the opposite side of the road, but again, none showed an interest in them, and they travelled along largely as the solitary moving car on the six-lane highway.

They drove onwards and the shadows slowly lengthened. The brightness of the sun remained strong and the heat of the day was comfortably balanced by a pleasant breeze brought about by their speed. They passed the many miles quickly with idle chatter and easy silences. Now and again at random intervals Kathryn would burst into song.

All this dropped off the closer they got to their destination and both of them became a little quieter. Gradually, James recognised things that they passed. A large silver water tower stood tall beside the road, surrounded by pine trees. It had a large dent on one side, and daubed in uneven and faded black letters were the words DEGG PAINTS INC. Farther on down the road they passed a small, simple church with a large bronze cross on top of a triangular roof, which glistened in the sun. They passed many turnoffs and multiple roadside banners advertising ADAMS' APPLE PIES and EMMA'S SHOE STORE – NEXT EXIT!

Though he had not been back in years, the familiarity of these landmarks still pricked James. With each memory evoked, the butterfly in his stomach beat its wings a little faster and he in turn became a little quieter still.

Finally, after many miles of travel, they came to the landmark that he knew best. The three lanes of the highway narrowed gradually into one and crossed over a large brickwork bridge high above a railway line. Trains had not run on the line for a generation. The rails were rusted and litter swept around the area. Thick foliage scrambled upwards all around the lines, and the plants were wildly unkempt and grew in random places. The bridge passed over the railway far below and stretched for around half a mile. This marked the final run to Pickering, leading directly into its centre just seven miles away. He took a deep breath, and his heart thumped a little faster and a little stronger.

This is it. I'm nearly home.

The road narrowed further and curved off to the left, descending slightly as they went. James slowed the car and carefully navigated the terrain. From the speed of the highway, it seemed now that the car was crawling through the country trails. The track spiralled through a forest with thick patches of trees that reminded him of Cedar Falls, and for a moment he was struck by the similarity between the pair of tree-lined roads. The light dwindled as the trees arched over the road, allowing only thin beams of light to pass through the leaves and branches. The air was still and the smell of the trees was sweet and rich.

Progress was slow and cars were strewn at regular intervals along the road. The gradual speed of their own vehicle allowed them once more to appreciate the damage and the carnage that the disappearances had wrought. Twisted metal and spilt blood were mixed seamlessly on a wrecked black sedan that had ploughed into a tree, splintering its trunk. The rear of the car lay at an ugly angle in the road and they did not pass it easily. They moved beyond an upturned small blue car that had a smashed window over a door that folded inwards. A torn scrap of cloth was snagged on a shard of glass, and James wondered if someone had crawled out of the wreckage. The car wheel crunched on the shattered glass as they rolled beyond it.

Is the person okay? Where did they crawl to? Did help find them in time?

After the incline dropped a little more steeply, James stopped the car. The road was no longer passable. Two cars had careered into each other, blocking the road completely. The front of a yellow estate crumpled into the driver's side of a navy blue saloon. Kathryn gasped at the sight of it, for the near side window of the estate was splattered in thick dark blood. He twisted the key and turned off the engine. They sat there in silence for a moment. No branch moved in the wind and no leaf floated to the floor. No bird sang in the trees and for a while, neither James nor Kathryn moved a muscle.

"There is no going around it in the car. We are going to have to go over or through the trees."

Kathryn did not answer for a second, but when she did, she spoke quietly. "I know."

"Listen, I had to do something similar when I came out of Cedar Falls. It's a horrible thing to do – it's someone's tomb –

but we must get to the other side. You can do it. We can do it together, help each other. Are you okay?"

"I'm fine, it's okay. Don't worry about me."

She was unable to take her eyes away from the wreckage in front of them and James spoke again. "Will you help me then? Please?"

"It's the first time I have seen anything like this up close. I knew that the disappearances would have caused terrible things – I knew that – but until now I had not really seen it. It sounds silly, but I never knew. The reality and the, what do you call it, the abstract? I think that's right. The abstract and the reality, I never really knew how different they could be. I was too busy having fun to notice."

"Take your time. There is no rush."

"No. I'm ready. I don't want to look at it a second longer."

Kathryn opened the car door and stepped out, closing it with a decisive slam. He followed her out and they stood side by side trying to work out the best way to pass. The decision was not easy, as each option had a discouraging drawback. Over the top of the mangled wreck was a risk, taking them across potentially unstable car roofs. To the right, the trees dropped steeply down, making any path through terribly dangerous. Kathryn made her choice quickly, opting for a route through the trees to the left of the cars. To travel this way, she first had to make a steep step upwards to the area which looked out over the road.

Kathryn scrambled to find something to hold on to but eventually clasped a hanging branch that cracked as it took her weight. The branch bent wickedly and although it creaked, it held, and Kathryn desperately pulled herself up between two trees. The gap between where she stood to the other side of the cars was only a matter of feet, but the density of trees was thick with protruding roots and drooping branches barring the way forward. There was no clearly visible route, and he watched as she struggled through, the wood scratching at her face and the branches slapping her cheek. It was dark in the foliage and she would barely be able to see. Kathryn stumbled over the roots and nearly fell several times, though the trunks steadied her path, and she was able, just about, to move forward.

As she went, James waited behind, and he could hear her make her way, though he was unable to see her through the trees. He heard twigs snap and wood crack. He heard her breath quicken and she let out quiet gasps of pain. Then he saw a blur of colour and Kathryn dropped down onto the road on the far side of the wreckage. He stood on his tiptoes and peered over the cars. Her face was red and her cheek had a couple of shallow scratches. Her hair was knotted and she was straightening it out. Kathryn turned her back to the wreckage and walked a little distance away to wait for him without looking back.

Weighing his options, James elected to take the same route and he clambered up the same area. In the darkness he crossed through the foliage, and in the closeness of the trees, his heart raced furiously. His steps were small and unsure but he tried to hurry although the haste and uneven ground made his steps clumsy and he stumbled onwards. Frantically reaching out, he felt for the rough bark of the trees, fumbling his way forward in a frenzied state. But, like Kathryn, he made it and gratefully leapt the short distance down to the road. He let relief wash over him and walked to where Kathryn sat waiting for him by the side of the road.

She was sitting down on a small patch of grass and James sat beside her. The road was winding downwards and the trees dropped sharply on the incline. She sat still just between two beams of light that pierced through the branches overhead. Her cheeks were now pale, her eyes unfocused and distant. From somewhere down below where they sat, they heard the trickling of a stream, though it was a long way away. The odd green leaf sailed silently down to the ground, floating and swaying as it slowly fell. He put his arm around her shoulder and guided her close to him, and she began to quietly sob, her body shaking against his.

As James held her, he looked over his shoulder at the wreck. Hanging out of the window of the estate was an unfurled arm leading up to a shoulder and a mutilated head. Caped in blood, the head had suffered an enormous trauma that had caused it to cave in one side, exposing the cheekbone. The jaw hung half detached from the skull, lying on the tarmac at an improbable angle. The flesh was scarred and tattered, in blotchy shades of blue and dull yellow, but it was the eyes that most unsettled him. The pair of grey eyes that looked unseeing at where they sat and through the blood, the crooked jaw full of damaged teeth smiling dreadfully at him.

Welcome home.

They had crossed the first major obstacle barring their way into Pickering, but it barely made him feel better. He felt a mixture of sorrow and anger that Kathryn had seen the wreckage. He had brought her here, and she should not have to see such things. It had been nearly a week since the disappearances, and still things had not returned to anything close to normal.

There are bodies in the cars. They are people. They are someone's daughter, someone's wife maybe, someone's friend, and they have been left here, alone and uncared for just as they were in Cedar Falls. No one had come to help them or give their body the respect or the dignity that they deserve, that anyone deserves. Things should have got better by now. People should have adapted and adjusted.

Kathryn should not have to see such things.

After a short time, Kathryn's sobs slowed and she moved away from his chest and looked at him through tear stained eyes. "How far away from Pickering are we?"

"About five miles, mostly downhill. I'm so sorry that you had to see that."

"It's okay. It is horrible, and I feel desperately sorry for them and the way that they have just been left here. But it makes you appreciate things somehow. There is no reason why that happened to them, but for the grace of God there go you or I. They were just so unlucky. I told you that I feel I have been blessed, and that just shows how fortunate we are. Domina called the disappearances an act of God, the Rapture. He claimed that those left alive were cursed, even damned. I think that we are the lucky ones and we have to make the best of it, however long we have left."

"I think that too. Thank you."

"Thank you? What for?"

"Are you ready to get going?"

Kathryn looked at him and seemed ready to say more, but she bit her lip and let the moment pass. Instead she contented herself with standing up and after drying her eyes with the cuff of her white shirt, she smiled and nodded. James stood beside her, and they began to trudge down the long road towards town.

twenty-two

The track continued to descend and eventually the tree branches retreated from hanging over the road, allowing the light maximum exposure over their walk. The sun beat down upon them and the way underfoot was hard and gritty. Droplets of sweat glistened on his forehead and the walk was difficult and uncomfortable. Kathryn took off her jacket and tied it round her waist, and he did the same with his sweater. The winding nature of the road made the distance from them to town seem that much greater, but eventually they came to the bottom of the hill and the track flattened out into one long straight path.

Stretching in front of them for a couple of miles or so was a long road that led directly to the outskirts of Pickering. A number of buildings on the edge of the small town stood out on the horizon. A church spire was the most prominent, but even that was not particularly imposing. For what Pickering lacked in stature the town made up for in terms of volume, and there were many buildings with a series of slated roofs bunched together. A large corrugate iron warehouse lingered just before the town limits closest to them, but the forklifts outside remained still and unused around stacks of wooden pallets.

From the view of the road, the town appeared remote, as all around the settlement were vast fields of green that encompassed all of the area up until the tree covered hills that surrounded Pickering. Although they were close, the unrelenting heat slowed their progress to a weary saunter. The tarmac of the road shimmered as they went, and the distant buildings were haloed with a lazy haze.

The afternoon had developed and the sun had long since begun to drop. As they moved closer to the town, he guided Kathryn to a narrow gap in the wooden fence that separated the fields on the left from the road they had walked on. Shaping his body through the space, he watched her follow, twisting her body between the gap in the fence.

"This is a shortcut. This was me and my friend's secret short cut. At least I like to think that it was secret. It leads to the centre of town. From there we can figure things out."

James ran his fingers through the tips of the long grass, carefully stroking the strands. The scent of the field was sweet, but somehow it smelt different to him from the grass elsewhere. He couldn't explain it, but it felt unique to him, and his heart unexpectedly ached. He looked at the town that he had grown up in.

I had forgotten its beauty. The long, green fields, the tall surrounding hills, the red brick of the houses. How could I have forgotten?

The strength of his emotion surprised him, but James welcomed it and let it linger inside him without pushing it away, painful as it was.

There was no direct path through the field, and it was clear that no one had walked this way in a long time. Indeed the route must have been imperceptible to those unfamiliar with the land. They were going to have to make their way directly through the long grass. Accordingly, they both trampled almost gleefully along as they went, and he felt his spirit rise, as did Kathryn, who giggled delightedly.

She stomped along and said cheerily, "I haven't done this since I was a kid!"

James smiled too, feeling again a sense of childish exhilaration as they continued to troop their way through the field. "Fun, isn't it?"

Across the fields and through the grass they went, laughing and joking along the way. The accident and the doubts were suddenly a long way from his thoughts. The sun seemed not quite as hot as earlier, the distance not quite as far, and their feet not quite as heavy. Eventually the field came to a horseshoe-shaped area of grey paved slabs. A number of streetlights arched around a large black wheel placed on a plinth. It had a brass plaque screwed into it that testified to the town's long abandoned industrial heritage. A series of backless benches were positioned around the wheel facing the road that lay beyond the paved area.

On the opposite side of the road was a long brick building with many windows, most of which were smashed and still others boarded up. According to the large white letters that hung precariously just beneath the roof, it had once been a tile factory. Ivy crept up and down the walls and nettles attacked its base. The damage to the windows was the result of long-standing dereliction that dated from before even his time, and indeed even in the many years since he had been gone, nothing much had changed about the building.

To many it was a monstrosity, an eyesore, but to James it was none of these things. It was a relic that was still important. The wheel was contrived, it was a manufactured monument to what had gone before, but the factory was a real thing. It was an authentic link to the past, and he was glad that it was still there. There was a rich context to it, and the building almost seemed like a living, breathing thing to him. It was an organic link from yesterday to today, from a life long ago departed to the present time in which they stood afraid and confused. James smiled to himself and felt a nostalgic feeling bubbling up inside. The wheel tried to provoke a sense of sentimentality that was brought about naturally by the old factory, and though the pride that he felt for his hometown was unexpected, it made him happy.

From where they stood, it was a short walk into the centre of town. Kathryn took his lead and they walked alongside an empty road. In spite of the carnage that they had seen on the outskirts of Pickering, it appeared that the cleanup operation was far more progressed in the town. Either that or the place simply had not experienced the disasters that it seemed to go hand in hand with the disappearances.

There were no shards of glass on the road, no railings were damaged and there was no sign of scorch marks anywhere. In fact, James observed, the place seemed clean, the old factory apart. The signs directed towards the town were neatly painted, as were the bus stops. As they came closer to the centre, he also noted that all of the businesses were intact. No windows were broken, nor were any of the stores whitewashed or vacant.

They walked over a road that flew across an empty dual carriageway below, and it led them to a small roundabout that they both crossed. A circular series of shops stood just outside the centre of town, curving around an area that they walked passed. There was an electrical store that continued to boast of special offers on surround sound systems and a unisex hairdresser with tinted windows that informed those who passed by that an appointment was not necessary. This scene progressed onto a row of shops that ran down one side of the road. Here was an eclectic variety of stores. A New Age shop displayed purple and emerald-coloured crystals, there was a health food shop with baskets of herbs and spices, a tattoo parlour had a large dragon sweeping down its window, and there was a small, greasy-looking cafe with a jolly-looking, fat gentleman painted on the sign. These shops were much smaller than the structure on the opposite side of the road, as a long and tall shopping mall stood covering a wide area of land.

The road that they walked down was empty of cars and people, but they both heard the low hum of others and they were nearby. The noise was not just close; it was plentiful in origin. There were people here in Pickering, many of them, and they did not sound as if they were angry or afraid.

They heard the buzz of people shopping. They heard the everyday noise of people going about their business. They heard the sound of normality. Crossing the road, they walked along the side of the shopping centre, turning right at the corner, where James and Kathryn came to the front and main entrance of the mall. They stood looking out from the mouth of the centre and gazed down the main street of the town. Dozens of people were milling around in the warm sunshine clutching shopping bags. Many others darted round rapidly gobbling pastries from paper bags as they walked. Others hung around idly, perhaps waiting for friends, casually leaning against railings and walls. Some people wandered about casually holding hands and looking into each other's eyes, barely conscious of where they were going or what they were doing. Handfuls of people were standing round talking and laughing amongst themselves. A man with a loose fitting blue T-shirt sold magazines, cheerfully propositioning all who passed him. Two men sold a series of potted plants that gave the street a colourful image and a sweet smelling air. Many people lingered around the plants, and James could see money changing hands. Bills were passed and change was given. He also saw that all of the shops were open, which, given the number of people out and about, should not have been surprising.

What he most marvelled about when he looked at his hometown at that moment was the sheer mundanity of the scene. It was as if the world had not changed at all, and it was truly a wonderful sight. The smile that lurked around the edges of his lips widened, and his heart leapt. Kathryn looked at his happiness and joined his smile.

"Well, what now, James? What shall we do today?"

He turned to look at her. "Let's go shopping. Right now. Let's shop. Let's pretend that the vanishings never happened and there's no purpose but to have a nice day and to get some lovely things."

Kathryn smiled. "I like to pretend. Come on, then. I like shoes. Do you like shoes?"

He nodded emphatically and offered Kathryn his arm. She took it, linking his with hers, and they headed off into the shopping centre, bouncing happily as they went.

The shopping centre was comfortably busy. There were not enough people to make movement difficult or restricted, but there were sufficient numbers to provide a easy bustling atmosphere of something that felt to James like a community. The warmth of the outside air was tempered with a pleasantly air-conditioned interior, which made for an easy time as they slowly wandered around the shops, taking their time as they went. For the first time since the disappearances, he felt comfortable with the people who were around him. Beyond the odd catching of another's eye, nobody paid too much attention to either of them, and everyone went about his or her business. The pace was gentle, and they did not rush as they idly moved from shop to shop browsing and perusing the peddled wares.

Together they thumbed through a stack of DVDs, laughing at memories of the comedies and reminiscing about childhood movies enjoyed long ago. Kathryn sang songs to herself from CDs she found, playfully thumping a smiling James in an unsuccessful attempt to get him to join in. He sat patiently as she tried on a dazzling and, what was to him, a bewildering assortment of dresses and outfits. She would come whirling out from a pale curtained booth, smiling and giggling, flamboyantly exaggerating her pose as she twirled in all manner of dresses and outfits. He smiled and laughed with her. She mused over shoes, and he studied a number of video games. Though much of the stock of the stores was diminished and remained un-replenished, there was much to spark their interest.

Thus far they had both refrained from buying anything as they moved across the various floors of the mall. A few of the shops were closed, but many were doing a fine trade. The patrons seemed unaffected by the events that had weighed heavily on James and Kathryn over the past week, and they seemed to move with a fresh and an easy air. There was a queue at the cookie stand and people sat on benches sipping milkshakes through a straw. But it was another outlet which commanded their attention, Kathryn's first, and she dragged him towards it.

They walked over to a temporary stall comprising of a table covered by a red felt. It was tucked away in the corner of the second floor away from the rest of the established stores. There were numerous figures placed upon the table created from a pale wood that was ornately and intricately carved to be shaped into a number of animals. The craftsmanship was detailed, providing amongst other things a carefully striped tiger and a curly trunked elephant.

Kathryn smiled at the man standing beside the table and knelt forward to gaze at the figures, which delighted her. She took her time, viewing a lion and a puma, an eagle, and a snake. She ran her finger over the wood and he watched her, her smile never departing for a moment.

Kathryn stood up and moved beside James. "These are wonderful! I like the elephant best. I had an elephant once. I say I had an elephant. I didn't actually have one in the sense that he lived in my garden. My uncle adopted me one for my birthday. He sent me a picture of himself playing in the wild and wrote me a letter every year."

James smiled. "An elephant wrote you a letter?"

"Yes, there was a hoof print at the end so I knew it was from him."

Laughing, James turned to the man who tended the stall and who was watching them with a hopeful smile. "These are great. Did you make them yourself?"

The man nodded. "I did. Thank you for noticing. Making your own stock is one of the only ways to make money since, well, you know. It's not like you can get on the phone and order stuff in or even draw money out of the cash point since all the machines are down and the banks are closed."

James nodded. "I was wondering where people had gotten their money from."

"Well, in some ways it is good, I guess. It is for me anyway. Everybody here who is working has to be paid in cash, and that money, rather than being stored or sent away somewhere, comes straight back out here. All the money that is made locally is spent locally. I find it kind of nice. I used to work at a ceramic factory and all the pottery that we used to make, and all the money that we earned, went elsewhere to people without any connection to Pickering. No one here ever saw it. I like that what is made here stays here. Local produce sold to local people. Everyone round here benefits, I think. I sound like a little town kind of man, don't I?"

Kathryn smiled. "Not at all."

"Thank you, young miss. I've been to a few places nearby with my stuff and many of them have been doing things differently since, you know. The stores in one town I went to was keeping a bundle of uncashed cheques, like tokens in transactions ready for when things get back to normal and the banks reopen. I thought that was pretty optimistic, myself. Another place seemed to be planning to do away with money altogether and had put in place some kind of bartering system and tradeoffs of favours. You can't keep people down, can you?"

Kathryn's smile broadened. "You certainly can't. How much is the elephant?"

"Because I like you, young miss, I think that ten dollars is a bargain. A steal! I am practically cutting my own throat."

James took out his wallet and handed over a ten-dollar bill. "It is a bargain. Thank you."

Kathryn thumped his arm. "I can pay my own way, you know."

"I know. It is just a gift to say thank you."

"Well, there is no need, because I haven't done anything. But thank you. I love it, I really do."

The man placed the money in a light brown leather pouch that was clipped around his waist. Reaching over the table, he carefully picked up the elephant, making sure that he did not knock over any of the other animals. Then he placed the wooden figure on white tissue paper and wrapped it up, sticking the top of it with tape. Following this, he slid out a plain white plastic bag and, caressing it open, dropped the elephant inside and passed the bag to Kathryn, who accepted it with a smile and a thank you.

"You are welcome. The two of you seem like nice folks. What are doing here in Pickering?"

"We are looking for someone, actually," James said.

The man paused for a moment, frowning. "Well, maybe I know where to look. Outside the mall is a notice board that lists the town's missing people on it. Everyone who has lost someone has written their name on there. Just follow the main street down and turn right. You can't miss it."

"Thank you."

"There's another thing. Find somewhere to stay tonight. Don't linger on the streets, please. Get yourself indoors."

Kathryn's smile dropped a little. "Why's that?"

"Please, just get off the streets by dark and take care. I wish you luck in your search."

Both James and Kathryn stared at him for a moment. She let out a small laugh, but the man remained unmoved. She looked at him for a moment longer and said, "Well, thank you and have a nice day."

Clutching her bag, Kathryn swung it to and fro as they wandered away back towards the main area of the shops. Neither of them spoke, but it was clear where they were going, and they walked with a purpose that up until then was absent from their time in Pickering. Crossing the mall, they stepped onto a moving escalator and descended to the floor below. They walked along the shopping centre, and the automatic doors of the main entrance breezed open as they stepped outside into the warm summer air.

They did not talk of where they were going, because they both knew the destination. They were heading towards the notice board.

twenty-three

the sun had deepened in colour, and the afternoon was progressing slowly, edging into the evening. There was still a warm haziness about the air, and the sweet smell of the potted plants continued to offer a pleasant sensation to James, even as he hurried forwards beyond them. Kathryn quickened her pace to keep up. They walked down Main Street, which, reflecting the modest population of Pickering, was not a lengthy path, though many shops were crammed side by side into the area. They walked passed a cobblers and a card shop until he stopped in his tracks beside a bar on his right.

Turning to look at it, James gazed in through the windows. The bar was a relatively new building, and he remembered when it was built.

I was just starting college.

He recalled the wooden frame and the scaffolding during the construction. He recalled the men working on it and the grand opening, which he had been too young to attend. It was a new building, but it was designed to look older. The bricks were a large marble colour and were dissected by black tinted windows on two floors. A silver handrail led two steps down to the front door, which was large and thick and created from the same colour glass as the windows.

But what caused him to halt were not the physical characteristics of the building; it was the emotional connection that he felt towards it. Since he had set foot back into his hometown, a feeling had sprouted inside of him that seemed to blossom with each step, even without him nurturing its growth. Each step that he took, each square foot of Pickering, carried some long forgotten memory that had awoken within him. His eyes darted about the street.

I remember walking down this way on a night out. I remember regular shopping trips here with my friends. I remember getting home early on an unremarkable day at college. When I was little I got a Mother's Day card from here with coins from my allowance jangling in my pocket.

A million random memories that meant nothing to anyone else made his heart ache profoundly.

Kathryn stood beside him. "What is it, James?"

He looked at the building next to them. "I came here with Danielle on our first date." He glanced to the left and pointed to a seat upon which a little girl sat licking an ice lolly. "I waited on that bench for her. She looked at her reflection in the window of the bar, and I remember her brushing back her hair ever so carefully."

Kathryn took his hand, interlocking their fingers. "Come on. Let's go and find out."

James lingered for a moment, staring at the bar, and Kathryn waited beside him. Then the door opened and a man emerged snapping him out of his thoughts and thrusting him back into the world. He mustered a weak smile towards Kathryn and they carried on walking. His nostalgia was moving freely from excitement to nervousness to fear as they turned right at the bar. They found themselves on a long street with a narrow walkway encased by buildings on three sides. Only small amounts of sunlight crept down along their route, and long shadows were cast down upon the red brick pavement. At the end of the street, just in front of the wall opposite the entrance of the path, was a procession of candles placed on the floor, one by one, flickering in the shadows. Behind this was a notice board with hundreds of small yellow notes attached to it. There was also a large black leather-bound book hanging on a chain and placed on a waist high wooden lectern.

The street was deserted, and only a few people passed by its head. He stood looking at it for a moment, then walked towards the book. Kathryn hung back and let him move forward by himself. He reached the board and looked at the notes posted. Some of them contained desperate words, pleading for information on a loved one. Other notes had only descriptions of people and telephone numbers. Some simply held words of prayer, neatly versed, asking for forgiveness and grace. Several begged hopelessly for a reunion between seemingly lost family members. A few photographs were pinned up of smiling children. One was of a little girl looking sweetly confused at the camera as she held onto a blue blanket. A single word was written underneath in bold capitals.

WHY?

James was struck by the sadness and desperation, the fear and resentment in this simple note, but also by the hope and defiance behind the sentiment. Many contained words of blessings for the town and for the country, and also for each other. There were words of encouragement and details of town meetings with the promise of survival, prosperity, and endurance. He moved from note to note, slowly reading the words and being struck by their intimacy and urgent longing. But he also felt a profound beauty in them and admired the steadfastness of the town's people to return to the semblance of normal life that they had experienced since they arrived.

Kathryn joined him and she too began to quietly read the messages, stepping carefully studying the desperate words. There were far too many notes for him to read all of them, and they were pinned up too randomly for him to approach the notice board in any kind of systematic manner.

Eventually, he picked up the book and opened it. The pages were laminated, and the first one contained black script explaining its purpose. James read the words intently and silently.

This book contains a list of those people taken from our town. It is a record of those that we have loved and lost, and although they are gone, they shall never be forgotten and will live in our hearts forever. This book cannot offer answers or even hope, but it is a testimony by those of us who are left in memory of those who have been taken. It is a sign of our determination to carry on together, even though we grieve as one body and one soul. God bless Pickering and God bless each other.

Following the opening words were a number of pages containing a simple list of people's names. The information was presented like a telephone directory and had one name per line, ordered alphabetically. The first page was headed with the title **THE MISSING.**

He flicked through the pages, seeking Danielle's surname, stopping at the letter R. His breath became heavier and his heartbeat quickened. James closed his eyes and the anticipation rose, along with the dread. The experience lingered. He was unsure whether he could release it. But the answer was in front of him. He scanned the reams of names slowly wanting to be sure and not to make a mistake. He traced the page down, feeling the smooth lamination in the tips of his fingers.

'RYAN, ADAM. RYAN, ADRIAN. RYAN, CHARLOTTE L. RYDER, CHARLOTTE T. RYDER, CHRISTINE. RYDER, DAVID. RYDER, ELLEN. RYDER, FRANCIS.'

James read it again and again. Repeatedly he scanned the same names until he was sure beyond any doubt. He felt the blood drain from his face.

The question was answered. Danielle Ryder was one of the remnants. She was here to be found, somewhere.

He waited for a moment. His heart slowed, and his breathing gradually returned to normal, though his emotions were still wild, his thoughts muddled. Eventually one thing became startlingly clear above everything else. He now had a decision to make.

What do I do now?

A plan of action is needed. A route, a path needs to be thought out. Danielle is here, isn't she? Danielle would never leave Pickering. She loved the town. But her family are among those listed missing.

She is alone here.

Maybe she's packed up and gone somewhere, like I have. Perhaps she has even left to find me.

Reason told him that was not going to be true. But the truth was that he simply could not know if she had left or was still here. The likeliness was that she was here when the disappearances hit. Months ago, one of the few friends he had who still lived in town had confirmed this, mentioning that he had seen her in the supermarket in the last email he had sent to James.

What if she got married? What if her surname has changed and she has disappeared after all?

There was no real way to know this, so he decided to carry on without acknowledging this possibility. The only thing he could do is work with what he knew and that was what the book suggested, that she had not vanished.

Finding her is still possible.

Kathryn looked at James. "So?"

He smiled at her humourlessly. "It's a list of people who are missing. Danielle's name is not here."

"Well, that's good. That's very good. What do we do now?"

His shoulders slumped. "I have no idea."

"Come on. Let's go and get a cup of coffee and think about what to do next. There's a cafe I saw on the way down here. I'm getting hungry and we can take our time. Let's go, James."

With that, they walked back into Main Street and crossed a short way before they stepped into the cafe. They placed their order and chose a seat and waited.

After a while, a waitress in a black-and-white dress brought two simmering cups of coffee in large white mugs to the small, square table where they sat. The cafe was moderately busy, and they had chosen a table by the wall in the middle of the shop. It was a franchise business, but a lot of money had been spent trying to make it look like it was not a chain.

There were brown sofas in the area at the back, and black-and-white photographs of local buildings in bygone eras were framed and hung throughout. Although it was sunny outside, not much light got into the cafe, and there was only a dim orange glow inside. A rich smell of coffee beans hung in the air and was coupled with a scent of freshly baked scones. There was a long counter upon which was perched a till and a glass cabinet filled with, amongst other things, pastries and sweets with thick chocolate chip and blueberry muffins neatly placed in a pattern. Picking up one of each of the muffins, the same waitress brought them on a small plate that matched the mug over to where they sat.

James sipped his drink. "They still have some coffee here then. I wonder how long that will last."

Kathryn picked at her chocolate muffin, removing the edges that spilt over the side of the wrapper and ate the rim of the cake as she went around. "I hadn't thought of that, probably not much longer." She nibbled a little more. "What do you think that guy meant when said get off the streets by dark?"

"Honestly, I'm not sure, but he probably just meant that it was dangerous. The crime rate is probably still pretty high what with the communication situation."

"That's weird, isn't it? No phones, no email, no television or radio signals. What's that about? Obviously it is connected to the disappearances, because they happened at the same time, and obviously what caused one has caused the other, but what the hell? Why have they not fixed it yet?"

"How can they? Nobody knows what caused either, and there may not even be a 'they' at all anymore. Think about it – no one can share information or summon help. Orders can't be passed down quickly across any distance anymore. Everywhere the chain of command has been localised. We are all isolated and alone, at least for the moment. Whatever, or whoever, caused the disappearances does not, for whatever reason, want us communicating with each other. They are clearly much more powerful than we are, so what can we do? It may well get worse before it even starts to get better. We are at the mercy of some other power. We can't see them, let alone stop them. They are unpredictable and powerful, and they clearly did not like the world as it was. They strike without warning, their motive is unclear, and their targets seem to be indiscriminate."

"Unless you believe Domina and the Rapture theory. In that case the vanishings were not random. Those taken were carefully selected targets. According to much of that idea, just being Christian is not enough. You must be the right kind of Christian. One with a personal relationship with Christ, as they say. And another thing, you are right about the warning that it may get worse, because if it is the Rapture, all hell breaks loose after that."

"For argument's sake, what if Domina was right? What hope is there after that?"

"Pretty much none. The story goes that after the Rapture, there is seven years left until the actual end. This is a time of increasingly severe judgments that are rained down by God upon the earth. The only hope for the remnants is to accept Christ as those taken did. Even then the outlook is bleak, as the beast emerges and murders most of the Christians for not taking his mark."

"The Beast? That's the 666?"

"It is, and nothing is symbolic in that doctrine. It's thought to be a literal mark, without which one cannot buy or sell anything. Those who don't take it will be probably be martyred, and those who do will be damned to hell for all eternity. Bit of a bastard either way, really."

"Are you still not convinced by it? I still can't believe it, though don't ask me for a better answer. I've still got nothing."

"Nope, I still love the world and can't believe God is so appalled by it that he wants to destroy it. Even if it is true and there is around seven years left, I want to go out having some fun. The final days of history? I want to go out with a smile, not with martyrdom."

James smiled at her. "I thought you might. What would make you smile?"

"Oh, I don't know, a Jolly Jumps jumping castle probably. You know the one, the kind you jump around and bounce on? My friend had one at a party I went to when I was a child. Even though I was really young, I think it might have been the most fun I have ever had. But right now we have more important things to worry about, don't we? What are we going to do now? You must have somewhere that you would like to start looking. How about her old house? Maybe her parents are still around."

"According to the book, her parents have disappeared, but their house is as good a place as any to start. They live in a cottage that stands by itself in an area just off a place called Rudyard Derry. It's only a short walk through the park to get there."

James sipped his coffee and nibbled a little more of his muffin. Though he had not eaten since breakfast, he was still not hungry, and he toyed with his food for a little while.

He paused for a moment and then spoke in a mumbling tone without looking at her, his eyes fixed upon his mug. "Kathryn, can I tell you something?" He blew on his coffee, and the heat reverberated back against his cheek, the warmth kissing his skin.

She too did not look up but answered in a soft voice. "Tell me later, James."

She brushed away the hair that hung across her face and tucked it carefully behind her ears, and then fixed her emerald eyes upon James and smiled. It was not a smile of joy or happiness, it was not a wide smile, but it was a gentle smile. It was a knowing smile of words unspoken but understood.

He smiled sadly back. He was not sure what he was going to say, but he yearned to say it anyway. There was a stream of thoughts in his head, and he might not get another chance to piece them together and talk to her. He longed to connect with her one last time.

Really talk to her like we have these past few days.

In as little as an hour I could see Danielle again. When I do, what I have with Kathryn will change somehow, even though I will try hard not to let it. What we have could slip away, and neither of us will say anything about it. It will simply drift away.

James looked at Kathryn and still smiled sadly, but he accepted her words.

I will tell her later.

twenty-four

by the time that they had left the cafe, the light had softened as the sun departed, making way for the moon. A smattering of vanilla raked across the land, stretching out above them over the horizon and across the deep orange skyline. The evening air was still warm, and a gentle breeze brushed across the streets, rustling the leaves in the trees.

They had not spent a great amount of time in the cafe, though they had eaten leisurely, but when they left the building, the town was deserted. The cafe itself closed the moment they stepped outside, locking and bolting the door behind them and dropping the blinds. The man with the flowers had packed up and gone away, leaving behind only some spilt soil, and the shops had closed their shutters. Litter swept down the walkway, a sheet of plain paper dancing and jumping erratically.

They turned left at the cafe and walked out of Main Street and away from the shopping mall. Kathryn's sandals slapped against the stone floor, and as the wind stilled, her steps were momentarily the only sound that they could hear in town that evening. Even the bar was closed, and no cars cruised the roads. Beyond the absence of people, James noted an absence of life, or at least signs of life. No light was lit inside any building, no glow illuminated any upstairs room, and no neon sign stayed bright.

The streetlights had flickered into life, but nothing inside any house added to the soft orange orbs.

They took a right at the end of the road and passed by a long paved area opposite a tatty row of low-budget stores.

James stopped for a moment. "When I was at college they put an ice rink here one Christmas." He took a couple of steps to his right. "And a big Christmas tree here next to it, with a star and baubles and tinsel."

Kathryn smiled. "That sounds nice."

"It was lovely. It was not a big rink, but it was good. Families skated on it holding hands. There was a guy who sold hot chocolate and candy floss right over there. Another guy sold Santa hats. You know, the ones that used to flash different colours? He used to sell reindeer antlers too, and stockings. Oh, Kathryn, he used to sell mistletoe. I remember."

James paused for a long time and stayed still, slowing his speech. "I remember."

Kathryn replied softly, "What do you remember, James?"

"It doesn't matter. Those times are gone now, aren't they? There won't be an ice rink this year, or Santa hats. We've lost it, haven't we? We've lost it forever. It has gone. All of this, it has all gone."

"You can't think like that, and you can't know that for sure."

"How can things be the same anymore?"

"They may not be the same, but it doesn't have to mean that things are not good. It does not mean that things are not happy or joyful. It just means that times may be different. Whether that difference is happy or sad is up to you. Just like it has always been. Now come on, which way is it from here?"

James looked at Kathryn for a while. "You're right, as ever. I'm sorry. I don't know what came over me. It is just over this way, through a few more streets and then across the park."

The route to the park was simple and straightforward. They crossed the junction of a deserted road at a double set of traffic lights. They walked downhill for a short while, moving beyond a mechanic's garage which stood beside a darkened fire station. Moving out of the shopping area of the town, they entered a residential region. Four large blocks of flats stood spaced out in a square shape in front of them, but James guided Kathryn to the left before they reached them.

The path they chose led beside a row of black spiked rails, which spread all around grassy fields with a black tarmac track running down the centre of them. The walkway was illuminated by old-fashioned lamps of a dim blue glow.

The evening light was rapidly failing as they entered the park. The deep orange sky had made way for a darkened blue, and long shadows were cast onto the path from trees that stood imposingly at various points in the fields. The wind picked up again and was chilly this time, rattling the branches and whistling through the leaves. The moon arched overhead, increasing in size and in its pale light, and it was joined by countless twinkling stars.

James looked around. Night was falling quickly, and it was getting late. Kathryn shivered beside him, and his instinct was to reach for her, but something held him back and they continued down the track. The sound of the wind was joined by a trickling of water from a nearby stream, and upon the horizon was the dark silhouette of tall houses with sloping roofs.

They were just about there. James touched his chest and felt his heartbeat through his shirt. His nerves sharpened.

They had walked in silence until they came across a children's play area. It was a simple plot. A pair of swings creaked in the wind, and the moon glinted off a metallic slide. There was also a seesaw and a roundabout, still in the darkness.

James glanced at them. "Kathryn, can we talk for a moment?"

"Sure, James."

213

They made their way into the play area before each took a seat on the swings. In the darkness they swayed gently together, slowly moving back and forth. Each was quiet, neither sure of what to say to the other, though each seemed dissatisfied at the lack of words. James grew reflective in his silence and considered his situation. The fields of the park were still well maintained, and the turf was neatly trimmed. The smell of freshly cut grass was sweet in the cold air.

It had been cut recently.

He sighed. Returning to Pickering had been a nostalgic homecoming, something that he did not think that it would be. He felt a love for the town that he had not known when he resided here. Despite this unexpected source of comfort, the search for Danielle continued to raise troubling questions. Now he was in Pickering. The vague plan and once distant destination was now a reality, but the hope and the practicalities did not square. Crossing a vast stretch of the country was relatively easy, despite what they had seen. There was always a route, a road to follow and a number of miles to steadily reduce. There was always a way forward and a certain absolute. The only question was where to stay from night to night.

Then they had arrived here, and he had found himself happy with where he was and who he was with.

But now I am here, what do I do?

The simple plan of action had been replaced with questions. Constant, unanswerable questions that he had suppressed because he had been so far away now replayed again and again.

Should I really try to find her? Does she want to be found? I have not seen Danielle for a long time, and on the last occasion I did, I hurt her so much. Did I break her heart?

Again the truth pricked him.

I broke her heart. So why am I carrying on?

The more that he thought about that, the more elusive an answer was. The sense of purpose that ignited the enthusiasm for the trip seemed a distant memory.

I'm no longer moving forward out of desire or happiness. No. I am moving now not for hope or expectation, but because I can no longer turn back. I have made my choice and am obliged to fulfil it, though I don't know who I am obliged to.

Now that they were here, again the question that overshadowed all others reared its head once more.

What do I do now?

He was so close. Her house was just over the horizon. He could hear the gentle trickling of the stream that ran just outside her window.

But he was tired, so tired. The numbness that deadened his senses in the immediate aftermath of the disappearances had gone. He took scant consolation. Sitting on the swing in the pale moonlight of his hometown, James felt the strain of the last few days. This was how he grieved for the world that he had lost.

Quietly, wearily, and plagued with doubt and fear.

Is Danielle the answer to my pain? Will she make it okay?

Kathryn seemed to sense his misgivings and smiled at him. "What are you thinking about?"

"I was thinking of something I was once told at school. I don't know why I remember it, but now I think of it, it seems strangely fitting."

He looked up at the night sky before continuing. It was now pitch black but for the sprinkling of stars and the moon.

"My physics teacher told me that the moon doesn't shine without the sun, and that when it is deprived of this light, it is robbed of all of its brightness. Without the sun, the moon has no beauty."

She nodded slowly and he continued. "I was thinking that if I could save Danielle, if I can save her, then maybe things will be okay. Maybe I will be able to salvage something from everything I have done and every mistake that I have made and all those hours I have wasted. If I can only help her, then the vanishings might mean something to me. At least then I will have made something from this whole mess."

Kathryn looked at him with sadness in her eyes. "James, I'm obviously getting nowhere with you. We have crossed the country, and you are still an idiot. You are so blind, I can barely even begin to talk about it to you. If you think that you need Danielle to give your life meaning, then there can be no hope for you. Why can't you see it? You are a good man. I believe that you are. I trust that you are. Why is it that you seem to think that you have done nothing with your life? Why is it that you think that everything you have done up to now does not matter?"

He looked at her quietly. A lump was in his throat, constricting his breathing that became choked. The hairs on his arms stood on end, and his heart raced. But Kathryn had not finished.

"So what if you never became an astronaut or a pro athlete or whatever you dreamed of being? What job you do does not define who you are. Your choices do – your thoughts and actions. It doesn't matter if people remember you, only what you do with your time while you have it. It's your kindness and your love. It's how you affect other people and how you let other people affect you. What matters is whose life that you, just being there, have made better. It matters who you have comforted, made smile, sang with, danced with. This is what defines who you are, not some job you do from nine till five for thirty years. Christ, James. It does not even matter if you find Danielle."

He looked at her, his tone angry in response. "How can you say that it doesn't matter? If that's what you believe, then why did you come? Why bother with the whole trip? You knew at the start where we were going and why."

"It was never about her! We have come so far, why can't you see it? Don't tell me that you have wasted your time if you don't find her, because if you believe that, then I have wasted my time, and I cannot accept that. You are constantly trying to see that which is just out of sight, and you go running after it and miss everything else along the way. Open your eyes. This is not a fairy tale. It's very likely that this is not going to end well. You are not just going to dance off into the sunset, and sooner or later you are going to have to deal with that. Then what are you going to run after? Save her, save yourself? You can't win this way, no one can."

Kathryn's voice slowed, and her tone became gentler. He saw in her eyes a sadness that hurt him. "It is a beautiful, wonderful life, James. The cruelty that we all see can be savage, even before the disappearances, is matched by aching beauty. It's everywhere. Please, please, open your eyes. I thought I knew what we were doing, but I guess I've made a mistake. I have to go. I have to pull away from you, because I cannot help you anymore. You're on your own now. I will remember these few days with you forever. Take care, James. I hope that you find some peace."

Kathryn slowly lent forward and kissed him softly on the cheek, and she got up from the swing, which continued to sway gently in her absence. Specks of red sand kicked around her ankles, and her brown hair brushed across her face in the breeze. Without smiling, she looked at him for a moment, and then she turned around and walked away from him, quickly disappearing into the enveloping darkness.

He sat and quietly watched her leave his sight without moving. Eventually her footsteps became too quiet, and the only noise he heard was the wind through the trees and the creaking swing beside him.

It grew colder, and as he sat there, James felt like he was a thousand years old.

twenty-five

the wind rushed against his face as he ran. Twigs crackled beneath his feet as he began to move at a rapid pace. His breath was frantic as he shifted from foot to foot springing over the grass, his arms pumping. The silhouetted scenery began to blur as his heart thumped faster and faster. As he ran, the worries and doubts ebbed away, and the questions that had so preoccupied James for so long no longer seemed so important anymore. He felt a freedom in his strides and an exhilaration flowing through a newborn hope.

Turning the corner he flew into Rudyard Derry, his eyes darting around. And then he ground to a halt.

At the end of the street, standing alone, was a house. It was darkly shadowed in the night, but it was tall and handsome, conveying a classical quality. Though he was over a hundred yards away, James could still trace its details. It had white walls with shoots of green leaves flowing up and down. Thick black beams supported the house and the thatched roof above. Facing the road, there were two windows on both the upstairs and downstairs floors.

A series of birch trees lined the road, and their branches dragged along the floor. The sound of a stream gently flowing was the only noise heard in Rudyard Derry at that moment.

The sole light was a soft glow from the upstairs of the lonesome house. It simmered from the upstairs of Danielle's house. He glanced at the glow, and for the merest moment, a shadow of figure darkened the light. Someone was up there, and for a split second they had looked outside at the street where he stood.

He remained stock still, gazing up at the window. His world spun, and he felt a weight in his gut. His breaths were deep, and his chest heaved.

After a while the figure returned to the window, and this time, the black silhouette lingered without moving.

That is it.

This is enough. James smiled. *It's done.*

Turning, he walked away from Rudyard Derry and moved back towards the park.

The hour was late, and the temperature was colder than it should have been at this time of year, so much so he could see his breath whisping in the air. James found his way to the play area and looked around. The dim light of the park and the thin slither of moonlight illuminated only a small part of the grass, and shadows blanketed the rest. He gazed out at the path Kathryn took when she left the swings.

He thought of her.

Her green eyes, her wavy brown hair, her smile, her singing, her dancing.

He thought of the way that they had held hands, tightly linking their fingers. He thought of the way that she had brushed her thigh with his, just for the merest of moments that night in the cottage. They had barely touched, but his heart raced. James thought of her words. He thought of each word that she'd said to him and the connections that they had forged, and he remembered every single thing.

Kathryn was right. It is a beautiful, wonderful world.

Amidst the chaos and uncertainty of what was around them, she had embodied the truth and endurance of her words.

She had made them real. She had lived them gloriously. But it was more than that.

I had lived them too in what little time I had spent with her.

With Kathryn, the promise of a new life stretched out before him.

James walked into the shadows and followed the route that Kathryn had walked, determined to find her, hope springing his steps as he went.

3822576R00127

Printed in Great Britain
by Amazon.co.uk, Ltd.,
Marston Gate.